I0766955

HOUSE AT RIVER'S BEND

RUBY JEAN JENSEN

Gayle J. Foster

CHAPTER 1

The house was only eleven miles from the highway in the valley, Mr. Pierce had said, but it seemed more like fortyleven to Jo Anne. In her small car she followed the man in the large car, and sometimes the dust blew full and thick and obscured everything. At such times Jo Anne dropped back, but she didn't dare lose sight because the road curled through the trees like a rope thrown carelessly, branching here and there as if parts of it had come undone. With no houses in sight anywhere, it seemed as though they had entirely left civilization, and she didn't want to be lost in the woods.

Only occasionally did she look around and then hurriedly. Always it was the same—black, leafless trees reaching ancient limbs across the road. In summer the narrow, rough road would be literally roofed and walled in green. Now it had the effect of a madly woven cage. Beyond the black limbs rose the dark green of pine forests.

The car in front suddenly turned to the right, going into the shadows of pines. The dust drifted away as the driveway became padded with pine needles, and she saw the stone wall, overgrown in places with perennial ivy, and the arched gate. With the dim sign: **RIVER'S BEND.**

This must be it, she thought as she turned the wheel, following through the arched ivy-grown gate. At first it seemed there was nothing but an endless mountain of pine. Then she saw the house. Set as closely into the pine forest as possible, it was nearly invisible. It appeared to be built of logs, its once varnished sides gone black now.

For some dumb reason she had gotten a picture of a house with white pillars and a veranda, like a Southern mansion. She leaned forward against the steering wheel. There was the porch, which he had called a veranda, going all the way around all right, at least as far as she could see, roofing out just under the second story like the brim of a hat. But the picture was not one of beauty. Instead, it was about the ugliest house she had ever seen.

"Well," she said aloud to her idling car, laughing at the contrast between her expectations and the real thing, "at least it's a house. Quite the large one too."

Jo Anne drove on and parked behind the other car. She saw then that the house looked as if it had been built on the edge of the world because there was nothing much behind it but open space. So that was the reason for this particular location: the view.

Mr. Pierce, of Pierce and Pierce, Attorneys, stood beside his car, grinning as if he had created it all especially for her.

"Beautiful view from here," he said. "Look."

She went to stand beside him and saw there was a backyard about ten feet wide and then a cliff with a nearly sheer drop. A few feet down was the tip of a stunted pine that had tried to find sufficient footing in the sparse soil on top of a lower cliff. Far below a river carved in the shape of a horseshoe wound through a green valley where cattle grazed. Several miles farther on the hills rose again, and beyond that the sky was pink and lavender where the sun was drifting below the horizon.

"Yes," she answered moving closer to the cliff's edge, "and a beautiful sunset too. I hadn't realized it was so mountainous here. The cattle down there look like puppies. It's an awfully long way down, isn't it?"

"I'd watch my step there if I were you, young lady," said Mr. Pierce from a safe distance. "Once you got started falling, there'd be no stopping you this side of the river. I always wondered why Mr. Stark didn't have a fence built there."

She came away from the edge and looked up at the house. "You said it is furnished?"

'It's just the way Mr. Stark left it except his housekeeper packed some things away. There's a caretaker, old Tom Willis, who's been looking after the place all these years. He's probably around here somewhere. I told him a few days ago that we'd finally found the heir and he said he'd have the house ready. He lives about a mile on down the road toward the river. But if I were you, Miss Stark—uh—Dodson —uh—I'd go back to town until I decided what to do with the place. I'm sure we could sell it."

A house of her own. A real house. "Mr. Pierce, I just couldn't do that. If my father's grandfather wanted him to have it, I couldn't sell it." Her eyes followed the low-swung porch up to the strangely boxlike top. The sun broke through the clouds at that moment and touched the logs, giving them a warmth she hadn't noticed in the darker pine-shrouded front. It was an omen, a welcome home by a family she had never known. "I've never lived in anything but a small city apartment. I don't believe I'll ever want to sell this house. I want to live here, where my dad was born."

Mr. Pierce wiped his face as if the cool March day was too hot for him. "It's not going to be very handy until you have it fixed up, miss. The house is heated by fireplaces and lighted by lamps. There's not even a telephone. You'd be living just the way people lived a hundred years ago."

"Well, if my great-grandfather liked it this way, maybe I will too. I think it would be nice to keep it the way he had it."

"If you do decide to sell," Mr. Pierce persisted, "we'll arrange it for you. My son is in the real estate business too. I know he'd be glad to handle it. I'll have to be getting back to town, Miss Stark—uh—Dodson? I can't remember that you're used to the other name. Anyway, you know who I'm talking to, I reckon. Would you like me to show you around the place before I go?"

"No, that's not necessary. I'll explore it on a warmer day."

"All right." Mr. Pierce' sighed. "But if you were my daughter, I sure wouldn't want you staying out here by yourself."

"Why on earth not? Isn't it safe?"

"Oh, it's safe enough, I reckon. It's just that it is a good ways to town. Eleven miles to the highway, fourteen to town. Have you got any luggage you want me to carry in? I wouldn't leave you here at all if I didn't know that old Tom is around somewhere." He had reached her car and was dragging three suitcases out of the back seat. Being a man of medium height and quite a bit overweight, the luggage, which he took in one load, set him to breathing heavily and cut off his one-sided conversation.

In the hush Jo Anne became aware of a sound she had not heard before. It was a low *oooo*, a soft and faraway moan, and it rose and fell again in eerie faintness. She turned, looking into the forest that crowded the front of the house, and its deepening shadows, but saw nothing. It was as though she and Mr. Pierce were in a world alone, and he unaware of the sound. She pulled her sweater closer to her body. She wasn't afraid of animals—but whatever that was didn't sound like an animal.

Mr. Pierce got a set of keys out of his pocket, unlocked a side door, and handed the keys to Jo.

The soft moan rose to a fine, singing wail, and still Mr. Pierce seemed oblivious to it. For sure now, it was no wild animal.

Jo could stand it no longer. "Can't you hear that?" she demanded in an undertone, as if her voice might draw its attention to them.

Mr. Pierce looked blankly at her. "I beg your pardon?"

"The noise. What is it? It's not an animal, is it?"

"You mean the wind?"

"It doesn't sound like wind to me." She looked up at the tree tops, but they stood like statues, sculpted in green. "There's no wind blowing."

Mr. Pierce grunted. "I can see you're not used to pines. Even when you can't feel the wind there's enough up there to set up a regular chorus. Especially up here on this mountaintop. Some people can't stand pine trees for that reason, but it never bothered me one way or the other. When you're in the house, it won't be as noticeable."

"I hope not. I don't think I like it." She kept looking up at the top of the trees, expecting a movement of some kind, but the trees were almost insolently still. "Are you sure it's wind?"

He laughed. "I'm sure. And I predict you'll be on your way back to town before morning."

She stopped hugging her sweater and shrugged. Nonchalantly, she hoped.

He held the door open and she went into a homey and comfortable library about twenty-four feet square. The books were still in the shelves on the walls, and the carpet, though old and of a blue-floral design, was clean and in good condition. To her right was a large fireplace built of native stone. A leather chair and ottoman, newer than the other furniture, sat near the hearth. The sagging seat testified to its popularity with someone. At one side of the chair a small round table held a tall lamp with a green shade. There were two doors other than the one through which they had entered. One to her left and the other straight across the room. The one to the left and the back of the house stood open. Through it Jo saw a buffet and one end of a dining table. The other door was closed.

Mr. Pierce said, "That's the door to the rest of the house, if I remember right. I haven't been here since old Mr. Stark's' death, twenty years ago. It opens into a hallway where the front door is and the stairs to the bedrooms. On the other side of the hall is a big living room and another room that I think was a music room. I was never in it. Just saw it from the hall when Mr. Stark called us out to talk about his missing grandson."

He dropped her luggage, went to the fireplace, and struck a match to the kindling there.

"I see old Tom has fixed you a fire," he said. "There's enough wood here to last into the night. He'll probably be around here after a while, before dark for sure. To see if you need anything else."

"The house seems to be clean."

"He's been paid all these years to keep it clean." He-touched the green-shaded lamp. "This is a gas lamp. Most of the lamps are kerosene. But this one burns white gas and you have to use a mantle on it. This mantle seems to be all right. If it gets a hole, it has to be replaced. Tom can show you how to light the lamps when he comes. This one is pretty complicated. I don't think I could do it myself, right off. Well, Miss Stark—Dodson—"

"Mr. Pierce, which is my real name? Legally, I mean?"

"It's hard to say, right off. Your dad being adopted by the Dodsons —still, there were no legal papers signed, relinquishing him for adoption. Legally, I'd say your name is Stark. But if you'd rather be called Dodson, since that's the only one you know—but still, legally, it's Stark."

"Then I guess I'd better get used to it. I never knew the Dodsons anyway. I've been so used to thinking of Dad as having no family at all that to find he not only had a grandfather, but a rich one, makes me feel—well—strange. But nice, you know? I'd like to know all about Great-grandfather Stark and his family. Dad's family." A moment later she added, "My family too. I can hardly get used to the idea of really belonging somewhere."

"I'd sure like to be able to help you, miss, but you already know as much as any of us. This place is pretty secluded, and the Starks kept to themselves. I didn't know he had a grandson until he changed his will and left everything to the child, if he could be found within thirty years. All he said was his daughter took the boy and left home. That's all he said. But you know all of that. We were about ready to give up and let the old Stark estate go to the charities when my son ran across those old orphanage records. Just why the Stark boy was left at the orphanage is something none of us will ever know, I'm sure. Nor will we ever know what happened to his mother."

"Mr. Stark must have been terribly lonely after his daughter and grandson disappeared. Poor old fellow."

"Yes. Well... if you take a notion to drive back to town, do you think you can find the way?"

"Yes, I think so. Thank you again, Mr. Pierce, for all you've done."

"No thanks needed, miss. We were glad to find you."

She stood in the doorway and watched his car move around the half-moon drive toward a different gate, then she quickly shut the door on the crying wind. Mr. Pierce had been right about the noise, not being so noticeable once the door was shut. One reason was the thickness of the walls, the door jamb was at least fifteen inches thick, and the window sills wide enough to sit on. The house evidently wasn't log veneer, it was solid log.

She supposed her father's grandfather, old Mr. Stark, had built the house. Although she had no way of knowing for sure, she estimated the house must be somewhere between eighty and a hundred years old, and the furniture, other than the leather rocker, looked almost as old as the house. All in all, the house lent itself to a feeling of peace and security, where generation after generation was born, lived, and died, with little knowledge of the poverty and struggle in the rest of the world. Someone had deliberately deprived her father of that security and left him instead in an orphanage. Why had he been cheated of his heritage?

Jo Anne warmed her hands at the fire, then left the library and went through the open doorway into the dining room. She went from there into a small hallway which led to a tiny room with a cast-iron bathtub, a sink, and a peculiar-looking old toilet with a square box overhead. A pull-chain hung from the box, so it must be some strange method of flushing the toilet, she decided. And in order to get the water up there in the first place it would have to be carried, because there were no water pipes at all in the bathroom. Not even the wash basin had a water faucet. Well. She had said it would be fun to live just like Great-grandfather Stark did, and it was getting funnier all the time. There was no window in this little room, and it seemed unnaturally dark.

She left the dark little bathroom hurriedly, opened a door that led to a bedroom simply furnished with an iron bedstead and a tall chest of drawers. A door from the bedroom let her into the kitchen. It too was a large room, as large as the library, with elaborately carved cabinets, and a sink of the same unglazed iron as the bathtub and wash basin. Beside it, like a big brown bug with an open mouth, was a rusty small hand pump that looked as if it would squeak to high heaven when touched. The opposite wall was almost entirely dominated by a monstrosity of a black iron cookstove. At one end of it a wooden box was nearly split apart under its load of chunks of wood.

Jo had never built a fire in her life, but she would have to if she wished to eat before she returned to town tomorrow. She had stopped at a grocery store on her way out of town and bought bacon, eggs, bread, and coffee with the pleasant anticipation of having a small, leisurely meal in her own house, before her own fire; but not once had it occurred to her that she would have to cook with anything other than gas or electricity.

There was little to do but wait for the caretaker, Tom Willis, or whatever his name was, to show her how to build a fire and where to build it. Jo Anne had wanted to see the rest of the house but the night shadows had crept rapidly in, and the thought of being in a house lighted only by one fireplace didn't appeal to her. For a wistful moment she wished her dad might still be with her so they could explore together. In the five years since his death she had not really gotten used to being alone. Even though this was her own house, and she had never been afraid of the dark in her life, she found herself hurrying to light the lamp in the library.

She found the lamp to be an attractive but alien thing. She could find no method in which to light it. She removed the green shade, found that the globe also was removable, which left nothing to take off but the queer little things Mr. Pierce called a mantle. It looked more like a doll's stocking to her. He had said it was necessary, however, and as there was nothing else on the lamp that looked as though it could be the source of light, she struck a match and held it near it. But nothing happened.

Darkness fell so suddenly while she fiddled with the lamp that the firelight created a black dungeon out of the dining room. She had wasted too much time. Having a vague remembrance of the location of the kitchen cabinets she ran through the dark dining room and into the kitchen where she began a hurried blind search through the drawers. She was about ready to give in and cry when her hand fell on a drawer that held nothing but candles. She sank weakly into a kitchen chair and leaned against the table. Candles had never struck her as anything to be overjoyed about, but at the moment she wouldn't have traded the ones clutched in her hands for another fortune. She found a candleholder, then went back through the dark to the fire-lighted library and lighted every candle. She found other holders on the mantle, and placed them evenly about the room. The light they gave out was very weak and fluttery, but it was light.

She sat down in the leather armchair, put her feet up on the ottoman and looked into the fire, listening to the snap of the burning logs. Beyond the sound of the fire seemed a kind of bottomless silence, the kind she had never heard before, and it made her comfortably drowsy. She leaned her head back and found the chair soft. She wouldn't have to get up in the morning to go to work, she could sleep as late as she chose, which to her was a luxury. Just exactly where she was going to sleep she hadn't figured out yet, but that didn't matter.

The important thing was that never would she have to get up and go to work. For her, life had turned out like a fairy tale. The poor little orphan girl, in tatters and rags, suddenly is found to be the king's lost daughter. The Princess of River's Bend.

Well, practically in rags. She didn't know what tatters were, for sure, but it sounded a good name for the small apartment she had just moved out of. It would also fit last winter's coat. And she might not be the king's daughter—just his great-granddaughter. And maybe not really a king—but rich. Oh, so beautifully rich.

A sudden noise brought Jo Anne from her reverie. She sat up straight and listened carefully. Had it been a door slammed? Or had it been a loud solitary knock? She remembered the caretaker, Tom Willis, and that he was supposed to arrive before dark.

Muttering, "Well, you certainly took your time," Jo Anne took a candle and went toward the closed hall door because there was no doubt in her mind but that the sound had been at the entrance door in the front of the house.

She opened the door and stepped into a long wide hall. The tiny flame on the candle gave out scarcely more light than a firefly, but it was enough to see the difference. The odor of mustiness was almost overpowering and cobwebs hung like long gray strings from the ceiling. Brushing them aside she made her way to the front door, but found it locked. It suddenly occurred to her that if Tom Willis did appear it undoubtedly would be to the library door, and her common sense told her that the noise she had heard was probably that of a limb falling from one of the trees to the veranda roof.

She turned to go back into the library and saw in the dim light the rise of a flight of stairs. Since she was there, she decided, she might as well take a peek and see if the upstairs rooms were as uncared-for as the hallway. And if they were, why? She raised the candle high, in a vain attempt to light the top of the stairs, and slowly climbed one step at a time. But on the fourth step she stopped, halted suddenly by the undiminishing darkness above, and an odd feeling that it had moved toward her. For the first time since she had entered the house she again heard the soft wail of the wind in the pines, and it sounded unearthly and voiceless rather than a realistic part of nature; she didn't like the sound.

Jo Anne stood still, looking up, feeling a cold draft on the stairway, in the darkness that seemed to be moving, creeping slowly down toward her, pushing before it the spider webs and the feeble light of her candle. That's silly, she thought, dark doesn't move. But she was all at once terrified, smothered as if by hands pressing on her face. Unable to take her eyes from the darkness she backed down the stairs, turned, and ran. As she turned the light on the candle blinked out, and by the time she stumbled into the light, warm, and comfortable library and had slammed shut the heavy door she was shaking so hard she dropped the candle.

For several minutes she leaned against the door and listened for a repeat of the sound, the knock on the door. For monstrous footsteps on the stairs. Anything to justify her running the way she had, like a silly coward. She wished she was back in St. Louis in her tatters and rags and had never heard of Pierce and Pierce or the mysterious family of Stark about whom not even the attorneys knew much. And then she wished she would stop wishing such junk and calm down.

She picked up the candle and tiptoed to the leather chair. She would go back to town, but Mr. Pierce would probably laugh himself sick at her, so she'd be damned if she'd go back before daylight. And where was that caretaker?

For the remainder of the night she sat in the leather chair, watching the logs on the hearth slowly burn away. She dozed occasionally, fighting sleep and listening as hard as she could. But to her amazement dawn broke with the awakening of hundreds of songbirds, and she was triumphant for having lived through the night. But she didn't think she wanted to spend another night alone in the house.

Her fear left, however, with the darkness, and as soon as it was light enough she again entered the web-filled hallway. It was oppressive and seemed alive with an invisible quality. She walked softly, but in the gray light of dawn it certainly seemed safe enough. She didn't go up the stairway again, but crossed the hall into an enormous living room that had two fireplaces and much old furniture. At the end of the hall she found the music room and in it a very old organ that no longer could make much sound. Dampness had overtaken the rooms, nearly mining the furniture and leaving the wallpaper hanging in strips. She finally summoned courage to climb the stairs again, all the way up, and found the bedrooms in the same condition. She counted six bedrooms in all.

Repairing the damage would cost an impossible amount of money, she thought. But then the remembrance of the money smoothed away her frown. Possibly, the furniture could be restored, and the house renovated as closely to the original as could be done. With that thought in mind she got into her car and left for town. And the first thing she was going to do, she thought, was say good morning to Mr. Pierce and tell him what a lovely night it had been.

CHAPTER 2

Three weeks passed before she returned to the house, but this time she came prepared. Through Mr. Pierce she had found Mrs. Alcorn, the plump middle-aged widow who had agreed to live in as housekeeper. Jo Anne would not spend another night alone in the house, at least not until she knew it from roof to basement. Of course she hadn't told Mr. Pierce that.

The interior of the house looked as though it had stepped back in time. The paperhangers and painters had completely finished the upstairs bedrooms and were working on the music room. The carpets had been laid, the bedrooms refurnished as nearly as possible to the original with many of the antiques that belonged there. A contractor had handled it so that she had spent a comfortable three weeks in town, selecting paint, paper, carpets, some furniture, and having more fun with it than she'd ever imagined.

The musty odor was gone, and the doors and windows stood open to the warm spring air. When Jo entered the house and looked over the rooms she felt that at last Jo Anne Dodson was gone, and in her place stood Jo Anne Stark. She had come home.

Mrs. Alcorn knew just what to do to make the black iron cookstove work, and took over the kitchen as though she had been born there. The stove sighed and cracked with heat, and Mrs. Alcorn put a roast into its oven for a slow bake.

Watching in amazement, Jo said, "You certainly know how to make that black monster behave."

"Reminds me of my mother's stove," Mrs. Alcorn answered. "There's no kind of stove made that cooks better."

Comforting sounds were all around, now. Voices of the workers from the other part of the house, Mrs. Alcorn's remarks as she looked over the old-fashioned kitchen. The total picture reminded Jo Anne of a kitchen from a Currier and Ives print. Nothing had been changed here or in the library or bathroom, except for the addition of more comfortable furniture in the library.

"The curtains do need washing," Mrs. Alcorn said. "I'll have to wash by hand. I don't mind that. Keep me busy."

The remark drew Jo to look at the window in front of her. She saw the curtains, dingy with time in need of a washing; but then her eyes were caught by a movement in the trees a hundred yards or more from the house, back in the deep shadows under the pines. Or it had seemed to be a movement. Her first impression had been that someone stepped out of sight behind a tree just as she looked out. She watched, waiting, but saw nothing and decided she had been wrong.

Just this side, though, was a building she had not seen before, nearly hidden from the house as the house was from the road by a heavy growth of tall pine trees.

"A garage!" she said, as the thought dawned.

"What?" Mrs. Alcorn cried nervously, nearly dropping an antique bowl.

"Oh, sorry. I didn't mean to startle you. It's just that I was wondering where I'd put my car, whether to build a garage. But there seems to be one here. It's so far back I hadn't seen it."

Mrs. Alcorn carefully put the bowl away and wiped her hands on her apron. "This kitchen needs a cleaning from top to bottom, just like I figured."

"I think I'll go out and look it over."

"I'd be careful out there if I was you. Could be anything in an old building like that. Snakes. Bats."

"Vampires and witches," Jo added, laughing. "Grief; You certainly are comforting."

Mrs. Alcorn didn't laugh with her. "I'd be careful. Why on earth a body would pick such a place as this to build a house is above and beyond me. I wouldn't be surprised if the whole building toppled off someday."

"You know, Mrs. Alcorn, that's what I like about you. Your optimism." Jo watched her, smiling. There was an air of distrust and gloom about the dear lady that reminded her of her old pal Dunrope, a bulldog that had lived to be nineteen years old without one single smile. Underneath his terrible outlook and aspect, though, was a heart as vulnerable and loving as a puppy's, if he liked you. Only those who didn't know him could ever take his terrible face seriously. Jo had a hunch Mrs. Alcorn was another Dunrope. And very possibly Dunrope reincarnated. Anyway, she thought she was going to like her. Since neither of them had a family, their arrangement seemed an ideal situation for both of them.

"Well," Mrs. Alcorn said, "I'd be careful."

Thinking it was rather nice to have someone concerned about you, Jo went out the door into the soft spring warmth and into the cooler shadow of the pines. How nice also to have not a care in the world. No money troubles, no nothing. Now she could be one of the idle rich and never have to turn her hand to anything she didn't want to do.

As the pine needles spread a carpet of silence under her feet, she drew farther away from the comforting grouch in Mrs. Alcorn's voice. The sounds of the workmen receded and as she drew closer to the shaded garage, she walked even more softly, as if an age-old instinct warned her to be quiet in this strange land. She stopped by the building, looking before she entered. The double doors at the front were closed, but proved it to be a garage, all right. At the side was a small door which opened easily. She pushed the door wide and bent forward to look through into the twilight of the interior. A black thing, spiny and dusty, forlorn with age, occupied a surprisingly small amount of dirt-floor space. She felt suddenly like laughing aloud, but kept it silent. The thing was an old buggy. No modern car had ever been driven into that garage.

She crossed the threshold and looked into the narrow seat of the buggy and touched it and wondered about the people who had ridden in it when it was new. This, then, she thought, would not have been a garage at all but a carriage house.

She brushed the dust off her fingers and moved quietly and slowly toward the rear of the carriage house. On the wall harness sets had mildewed green. She had seen enough Westerns to recognize them as harnesses, but beside them hung strange old items she couldn't identify. On the long workbench lay piles of rusted tools, hammers, wrenches, small piles of nails rusted into permanent little heaps. On the floor beneath the bench a large pile of old chain brought to her mind Mrs. Alcorn's caution about snakes. Somewhere in the wall came a quick movement, a rustle of a small animal as it hurried away from the intrusion.

Jo left through another small door in the rear wall that was standing partway open. She stepped through quickly and quietly, and looked up into the eyes of a man standing just a few feet away. Standing as still as the pine at his side. Her breath caught and her hand went to her mouth to stop a desire to scream. It seemed that nothing in the world was louder than the pounding of her heart.

He stared at her—or at least his eyes didn't move away from her. She stared at him. Openly. Fixedly. Unable to do anything else. His skin was so deeply tanned it seemed at first that everything about him was black. His hair, his eyes, his shirt, and his trousers. And he might have been the Devil himself for the tremor he raised in her.

Her hand pressed harder to her throat and the pounding pulse. She tried to slow it, and made a great effort to hide her uncertainty. She couldn't run. She felt if she moved, turned, or took her eyes off him he would reach out and she would be gone, food for the Devil's soul. No mere human could be so powerful nor so handsome.

To her amazement he moved and became human. He took one step backward. "I'm sorry," he said, a voice that fitted him, deep and masculine. "I scared you."

She licked her lips, but for once she couldn't smile. "I wasn't expecting to see anyone here."

"You don't mind, do you?"

A smile put the finishing touch to his strongly handsome face. But it seemed too perfect, as if it were professional, with a purpose other than simple friendliness. She couldn't respond yet. She felt herself backing away, coming tight against the garage wall.

"Mind?"

"If I look around. Maybe I should explain. . ."

For the first time his eyes left hers to glance down, and he reached up and brushed at his hair. A gesture that suggested he wasn't as confident as he looked. "I'm Loren Richards, a writer. You see, I know who you are. Your story was in the papers within several hundred miles, and I couldn't help being extremely intrigued by it. Since I'm a freelancer and can go where I choose, I decided to come down. I got here before you did, and I'm camped down by the river. The cliff isn't as endless as it looks from your backyard. The hill slopes on there a ways, and there's a path down to a nice little beach. Of course, the road goes by there too, but that's three miles around, so I just use the path." He looked up with his smile back in place. "I do hope you don't mind."

She wasn't so sure that she did mind. The tremor in her body had changed to a dull thud of some kind that she didn't recognize. An after-effect of being scared half to death, probably. "You've been looking around for several weeks, then."

"Yes. Four to be exact."

He had a businesslike abrupt Northern accent that sounded cold.

"But why? What are you looking for?"

He motioned vaguely. "The story was—well, unbelievable, too incredible, you know? I wanted to know more about it. When I saw the house I had to stay. And of course I wanted to meet you."

"What do you mean about the house?" Though she was slightly Southern she could be abrupt too if she tried hard enough.

"It has an air about it, you know."

"No," she snapped, feeling anger replace the peculiar thudding of her pulse, and glad of it. "I don't know. It's just a house. And you're a trespasser."

"I know," he answered. "But I give you my word I did not enter the house. Scout's honor. I looked through a window, that's all. And I haven't bothered a thing. I wanted to go in, but I didn't."

"The house was locked."

A look of faked innocence passed over his face. "Was it? Oh, I'm sure it was."

She thought as she faced him with new bravery that he was either the Devil as she had first suspected, intent on sucking her soul from her as a black widow would a fly's, or he was telling the truth. And if it were the truth, and he was merely a curious writer, then he only succeeded in raising her own curiosity.

"Then what are you looking for?" she asked again. "A story?"

"A writer always looks for a story." He came toward her, his hand out as though to guide her back toward the house. Before he could touch her though she turned, and he fell into step beside her.

"Were you on your way to the house just now?" she asked.

"Well—actually, no. I had in mind the same thing you did. Going through the garage."

"Oh, would you like to see it?"

His hand touched her back lightly, and her flesh tingled. "I'd rather see your house. You are Jo Anne Dodson, aren't you?"

"Yes. Only the name is Stark."

"You're already using the Stark name?"

"Of course. Why not? It is my legal name."

"How can you be sure? Were the records at the orphanage that complete?"

"You read the story in the papers, you said." For some reason his questions annoyed her.

"Yes, but it didn't give enough details. I was just wondering exactly how it happened to take twenty years, or perhaps longer, to find the Stark heir."

"There's no secret that I know of. My father was left in an orphanage when he was about fourteen months old, and his name was given as David Stark. That was all the information they had. It was a small home, run by an old lady, and the records were in a box, they said, and had been for years, since the orphanage was closed. My dad lived there until he was thirteen, then a couple named Dodson adopted him and took him to work in their store."

"And then?"

"He stayed there in the store until he married. Then the Dodsons died, and later his wife died. That was his first wife, you see. Then he married my mother. She died also, in childbirth, when I was only ten."

"I'm sorry. The child must have died too, since you have no sister or brother."

"That's right."

"Your mother had no relatives either, I understand."

"Right again. She came from an orphanage also."

"And then you lost your father when you were barely eighteen, so that you were all alone in the world."

His sympathy embarrassed her. "Well, yes. Except for Dunrope."

"Dunrope?"

"Dunrope was my dog."

The glance he gave her then was wordlessly compassionate, and she turned her face away. Pity she had never wanted. But then she wondered if the sympathy in his eyes was as professional as his smile, and thought it must be if he were a newspaper reporter out after news. She decided to volunteer all the information and be done with it so he could take his story and go.

"The first I knew about the inheritance," she said, "was a letter from these attorneys asking about my dad. I wrote all I knew. About two months later another letter came, asking me to contact a certain lawyer in the city where I lived. So I did, and all he wanted was proof that I was my father's daughter. So here I am." She smiled up at him, fully relaxed now that they were nearing the house. "I'm afraid there isn't much story there."

He smiled too, not quite as brightly as she. "If you'll pardon me for asking—there is a lot of money involved, isn't there?"

"Yes. Much more than it would seem, seeing how Great-grandfather Stark lived. He didn't spend much of it."

"And you, will you be able to spend it as you please?"

"Mr. Pierce said I could, even though he has to approve anything I want until I'm twenty-five."

"I see. On your twenty-fifth birthday you come into full control."

"Yes."

"I believe you have a couple of years to go yet."

"I'm almost twenty-three."

"Well!" he said, sounding as if he had drawn a long breath. "How do you feel?"

"Feel? About the inheritance? Oh, gee." She looked off toward the horizon where the blue sky floated white little clouds. "Fabulous. Like Cinderella or some other fairy-tale princess. All of a sudden I have a family. I have everything!" After a hesitation she added, "And kind of scared too."

"Why were you scared?"

"Because. . . ." She searched for the answer she hadn't defined before. "Changing my name was like changing my personality. Becoming someone different from me. I wasn't sure I could."

"Did you?"

She looked up into his dark eyes, but dropped her glance quickly. His eyes seemed too penetrating, like his questions. Too eager. Somehow like a cat's whose gaze is fixed on the promising exit. She wasn't sure she believed his reason for being there.

She asked, "What did you say your name is?"

"Loren Richards."

She stopped by the porch, one hand feeling the satin finish of a cedar post. "Mr. Richards, I've told you all I can. I'm sorry. What newspaper did you say you were with?"

"I didn't say I was with a newspaper, Miss Stark. I said I was free-lancing. And if you'll pardon the dispute, I don't think you have told me everything."

His smile hardly tempered his words. She stared at him.

He added, "Everything you think is important, I'm sure. But hardly anything at all. In fact, I'll bet I know more than you do."

"What?"

"I'll be glad to tell you when there's less interference." He raised his face to the wind and took a long breath. "Someone around here is a very good cook. Mrs. Alcorn, no doubt."

"How did you know her name?"

Before he could answer, had he been going to answer, which Jo Anne was not at all sure of, Mrs. Alcorn stepped through the kitchen door. If she recognized the man, she gave no sign. She merely gave him a long once-over and then turned to Jo.

"Pardon me, Miss Jo. You've got company in the library." Her attempt at concealing her own opinion failed, and she said contemptuously, "Some old man."

"That must be Mr. Willis, the caretaker. I've been wanting to see him. Excuse me, Mr. Richards."

"Loren," he said, but she was already going into the library.

SHE SAW the back of a thin old person who was dressed in baggy overalls and a gray shirt. He was standing quietly in the center of the room, his hat in his hands, looking into the newly painted and papered hallway. His head moved from one side to the other as far as his neck would stretch as though he aimed to see all he could without moving. Jo Anne interpreted his actions as timidity.

"Go on in and look around if you want to," she said gently. Elderly people always made a softie of her. Probably because her own father hadn't been very young when she was born, and the weight of poverty had made him stoop early so that he seemed even older than he was.

The man jumped as if she had given him a kick in the seat of the pants, and swung to face her. His blue eyes, set like little peeps of a pale winter sky in his shriveled face, blinked rapidly at her.

"My land, you're no bigger than a minute. Why you're just a young little thing. I figured you to be older."

"Uh—my father was pretty old when I was born."

He nodded, changing the subject quickly as if his first words had been unintentional. "Looks a heap different around here. In there, I mean, don't it?"

"Yes. You're welcome to look the house over, if you'd like. It sounds like the workers are leaving. They've probably finished."

"Much obliged, but I reckon I'll just stay in here." He stared at her as penetratingly as the writer had, and after a moment said, "So you're Mr. Stark's great-granddaughter. I'm pleased to meet you miss. I'm Tom Willis. I live a piece down the road yonder, towards the river. I've been working around the place here most of my life. I keep wood cut and packed up, and whatever else needs to be done. I ain't as strong as I used to be so I don't ask much pay."

"Most of your life?" she repeated. "Do you mind saying how long?"

"Don't mind at all. When you get to my age, the years mount up so fast you lose track. Let's see. I was borned in eighteen-ninety-three and I started doing odd jobs for Mr. Stark when I was big enough to stack wood. My pa, he worked up here, so he just kind of brung me along. I stayed after he passed on of a summer complaint."

They sat down, the old man relaxed and leaning back, Jo tensed and leaning forward, her elbows on her knees. Here was someone who had known her family.

"You remember it well?" she asked eagerly. "Those days, *I* mean."

"Right well. Looked pretty much like it does now. Mr. Stark used to set at that there library table in the corner, readin' and scribblin'. He could near always be found right here in this room."

"Then you knew my grandmother, didn't you? And you probably saw my father too. He was born in nineteen hundred."

Tom Willis's head had begun to shake before she finished her question. "Never saw no baby. Never even heard tell of a baby till about a month ago when Mr. Pierce, that there lawyer, come out and told me he'd found you. You could have knocked me down with a spit of 'baccer juice when I heard old Mr. Stark had a grandson. They said it was in his will, but then I never seen his will, even when he died, twenty years ago."

Jo frowned, mentally counting. "Well, you would have been only seven when Dad was born. You might not remember that. You must have known something about my grandmother, though. Do you remember her?"

"Which one was she?"

"Which one? What do you mean?"

"Mr. Stark had two girls. I was just a wondering which one of the girls borned the child."

Jo felt as if a cold, hand had been laid across the back of her neck, and she had no idea why. The chills crept slowly down her body. She sat back so that her head rested against the back of the chair.

"Mr. Pierce didn't tell me there were two. One was all I heard about."

"No, they was two. But both was gone when I started working for Mr. Stark. I do recollect seeing them once—in a buggy with some young feller. One girl was real pretty. But I don't know which one took the baby and left. I recollect the funeral because I come along with Pa when he dug the grave. It's right here on the place. Back in them days, you know, they didn't have these dadgummed silly laws. You could bury a body wherever you wanted. So the grave is right out yonder, north of the house, in a little clearing in the pine."

"What funeral?" she whispered.

'The girl that died." He must have anticipated her next question because he jerked his head back toward the north, in the direction opposite the carriage house. "Her grave is out there, not a hundred yards from the house. I recollect the day of the funeral. A hot summer day. And it was about that time that the other girl left, I reckon, because she wasn't there. They wasn't nobody there but me and Pa and another man who helped lower the casket, and old Mr. Stark and his housekeeper. But I didn't know one girl from t'other, and I don't know if it was the pretty one that died, and I never heared tell of no baby. And Mr. Stark, he never mentioned no names to me, and I didn't ask him no questions. He was a fine old chap and lived to be ninety-six years old. Never had nobody around but me and the woman that kept house and looked after him. Since he died— and that's been twenty years—I've tried to see that nobody stole nothing. Had a few prowlers, so I finally brung my cot up here and lived a few months. Never had no more trouble with prowlers." He paused and looked toward the central hall. "Stayed in this room," he said in a lower voice. "After a while I shut that door there and never went past it. I reckon things got in pretty bad shape in there. Nearly twenty years is a long time to keep a house closed up."

"I was wondering why that part of the house was ignored."

"Oh, I didn't ignore it, Miss Stark. I just didn't go in there. Is your housekeeper woman aiming to stay here tonight?"

"Yes."

"Well, I'm pleased to hear that, Miss Stark."

"My name is Jo Anne, but I like to be called Jo."

"Where do you aim to sleep?" he asked, as if she hadn't spoken.

And then he waited, almost without breathing she thought, for an answer. She frowned her surprise and annoyance. Even though he was over eighty years old, she didn't know if she liked such interest in her bedroom.

"Upstairs, naturally."

'Where at?" he demanded, leaning toward her.

Jo instinctively drew back. His actions puzzled her and she found herself wondering if he had all his marbles. "What difference does it make where I sleep?"

"Might not make none, but I'd be careful if I was you. Mr. Stark used the northwest bedroom, died in it. I always had a feeling about rooms people died in. Why don't you use the bedroom down here?"

"The bedroom downstairs is Mrs. Alcorn's room. I had no plans to use the northwest bedroom anyway, but not because of—of a death. I—well, gee whiz, Mr. Willis!"

But then he leaned even closer and she realized his mind was not traveling with hers.

"I ain't superstitious," he said in a lower voice, "and I don't believe in ghosts and hants and truck like that, even if I do have a feeling about rooms where people die, but I'll tell you one thing that you ought to know. There's something that ain't right on the other side of that there door. I heared things in this house I ain't never told nobody, and never figured to, but when I seen you, just a hundred-pound youngster—"

To her consternation he stopped and just looked at her. "Yes?" she said.

"Well—" he squirmed, twisting sideways— "you'll probably think I'm just a crazy old man. And maybe I am."

"No, I won't," she said. "I promise. Please tell me." She wouldn't be able to rest until she knew what he had on his mind.

"Well." He drew a deep breath and faced the door to the bright hallway. "I first thought it was a dream. I had my cot set up right about there by the winder so the breeze could blow in on me, and I had all the doors open, includin' the one to the hall there and the front door. It was early July, and hotter than—well, hot. I went to sleep, and long in the night I come awake like somebody had yelled in my ear. But after I was wide awake I never heared a thing except a screech owl somewhere in the woods. I never would have thought no different but that it was a land of nightmare, if it hadn't happened again. That next time, though, the night was chilly and I had all the doors and windows shut. Just like before it was like someone said something in my ear. It woke me fast. But then I couldn't hear a thing but the tick of the clock. I decided to see what I could find, though, so I took me a lamp and went to the hall and. . ."

She waited without saying anything, and a moment later he went on.

"Well. You might figure me to be a crazy old man, but it's a fact I never had such a feeling in my life. I was as stiff as that cheer you're settin' on and I couldn't move. I was halfway up the stairs and I never felt so odd in my life. It wasn't right. I was cold as ice. I didn't see a thing. When I could finally move, I was so scared, I came back in here, shut that door, and never opened it again, except once. I've shore never figured it out."

Jo thought of her one night in the house, and the almost wild, unreasonable feeling of fear. "That's strange."

"You probably think I'm just a crazy old man."

"No, I don't. Because I felt that same way the first time I went into the hallway. Probably because it was dark and spidery."

"It wasn't spidery when I was in there. Some things ain't meant for a mortal to figure, Miss. The human mind couldn't stand it. Anyhow, a few nights later the same sound woke me. But that time I didn't budge. The next morning, though, I went upstairs and searched all the bedrooms and didn't find a thing. After that, though, I began to hear it so often I thought I was—well, anyhow, I moved back to my own house. That's why I shut that door and never opened it no more."

"You say a sound kept waking you. What was it?"

"Now that's the craziest part. It sounded like a newborn young'n. Did you ever hear one cry?"

Jo shook her head. "No, not a newly born. Three weeks—"

He interrupted. "It's like a gasp, as near as I can describe it. There's other things that sound something like it. Baby lambs, for one. So all I know is I must have heard an animal and mistook it." He got up, holding his hat in front of him again. "But I shore am glad you don't aim ta stay here alone. If you ever need me at night, just come out to the road and start runnin' down the hill towards the river. I live in the house between here and the river. And I reckon I'll be around somewhere in the daytime if you want me."

"Oh. Yes. Just go ahead as always, as long as you like."

She got up after a moment and followed him to the porch. She heard him say, "Well, howdy there. Did you finally get to meet Miss Stark?"

The writer was leaning against a post, his arms crossed, looking comfortable and at home. She had forgotten him and also had forgotten how beautiful he was. She thought he should have been a model, but thought too with a personality as snoopy and pushy as his he was probably in the right business. His good looks probably helped him out, especially where women were concerned. She made a mental note not to let him influence her in any way she didn't wish to be influenced. A new thought struck her—one she hadn't really been able to absorb. She was now a very wealthy girl, a great prospect for a good-looking, gold-digging bachelor.

CHAPTER 3

Behind her Mrs. Alcorn said. "You want to eat now, Miss Jo?"

Jo started to turn, then thought it wouldn't really be polite not to invite the writer since he was there and since he had already mentioned the good smell of the food. And he really looked as if he could stand a good meal. She looked around for Tom Willis too, but he had already disappeared.

As if he had read her mind Loren Richards unfolded his arms, and backed a few steps away. "Excuse me, it's your lunchtime. I'll run along. If you don't mind, I'd like to look through the carriage house."

She nodded, giving him permission. It was better than inviting him to eat, she thought, not knowing any more about him than she did and without telling Mrs. Alcorn in advance.

She went in to find that only one place had been set.

"Aren't you eating, Mrs. Alcorn?"

"I can eat later."

"Oh, bosh. Here, I'll get your plate myself. I've eaten alone for years, since Daddy died, and that's too long. I want you to eat with me. I almost invited that writer to eat too. But I thought I really should ask you first."

"You can invite anybody you want. But I'd be careful about that dark one if I was you."

She sounded so dire, as if she had just pronounced a terrible sentence or made a disastrous prophecy, that Jo stopped and looked at her. "Why? Do you know him?"

"I never saw him before. But there's something fishy about him if you ask me. I kept my eye on him while you was talking to that crazy old man, without him knowing it, and it looked to me like he was listening to every word you spoke."

Jo smiled. "I don't doubt it. He claims to be a writer, you know, and he seems to think there's a *story* here somewhere."

"A writer? A story! Is that what he said?"

Jo giggled softly to herself and thought of Dunrope and his eternal suspicions. He had even suspected the mailman of treachery just because he came at a certain time every day. Dunrope always waited at the door, growling, and then sniffed the mail that fell through the slot to make sure it was safe.

"Yes," Jo answered, "that's what he said."

Mrs. Alcorn snorted, and filled her plate.

After a moment of silence, Jo asked, "You've lived here a long time haven't you, Mrs. Alcorn?"

"Quite a while."

"Maybe you heard something about the Starks."

"No. I always lived in the valley. Never had been up this way before."

They had hardly finished eating when a brief knock at the door was followed by a new face. On the young side, yet definitely mature, smiling and friendly, he didn't wait for an invitation. Even as he said, "Is it all right if I come in?", he came in.

He crossed the room holding out his hand, and Jo put her hand in it. He squeezed it between his palms and held it, smiling down at her.

"Dad didn't tell me how beautiful you are, Miss Stark, or I think I would have been here sooner. I'm Dan Pierce, in real estate, as well as law. I'm the one who located your father's records. I actually came out to look the place over and see if you want to sell it." He didn't seem to expect an answer. He turned his smile on Mrs. Alcorn.

"Hello there, how are you?"

"Well, thank you."

Jo was surprised to see that Mrs. Alcorn nodded and smiled. A tight little smile, but a smile.

Dan Pierce squeezed Jo's hand again and said intimately, "I've known Mrs. Alcorn for years. She's a fine person."

"Pshaw," said Mrs. Alcorn.

He released Jo's hand at the point when he could have held it no longer without claiming it as his own, and she murmured, "Yes, I agree. Although I haven't known her very long. As a matter of fact, your dad recommended her as the best housekeeper I could ask for."

"I think we're causing Mrs. Alcorn to blush. Maybe we'd better get out of her kitchen." His attention was suddenly on the room, and he hardly paused to draw a breath. "This is an interesting old kitchen, isn't it? Interesting house and location. Antique lovers would go wild here. I'm sure we could easily sell it for you."

Still talking, still looking, he went through into the library, peeked into the hallway, then back into the library, Jo following behind him.

"Say, this is interesting. Quite a lot of books. As old as they are, there are bound to be some valuable books here." He drew one down from a shelf and blew the light layer of dust away. He glanced at the tide, then looked at Jo. "Do you know anything about old books?"

"Nothing," she said. "I know so little I hadn't even thought about them being old."

He nodded. "Don't let anybody borrow any of these until you've checked them out for value."

"I'll try to remember."

He put the book back and went to stand on the veranda. "It's a lovely place considering—" His words stopped suddenly, then he said, "Who's that?" And his tone had changed, sharpened so that Jo glanced at him in curiosity. Then her eyes followed his.

The writer was coming out of the carriage house by the small door at the side. He turned, saw them, and waved.

"He's a writer," Jo explained. "Camped down by the river. He asked to look at the garage."

"Do you know him?"

"No, I've just met him."

Dan Pierce was no longer smiling and friendly. He started down toward the garage. "It's because of me that you're here, because that old will intrigued me and I kept digging at it, and I feel responsible for you, Jo Anne—can I call you that?"

"Just Jo, please."

"Jo. Thank you. It fits you. But listen, Jo, you've had too much publicity and you know how publicity attracts all kinds of characters. We tried to keep it out of the papers, but weren't too successful."

"He's the only stranger who's come around to my knowledge."

"One's enough. One is all it takes."

They met in the path. Jo automatically compared the two men and noticed how straight Loren Richards carried himself. He was tall enough that he looked down at Dan Pierce, and he looked down arrogantly, it seemed to Jo. Although Dan Pierce was presently in very good shape, he would probably be like his father someday.

"Dan Pierce, Loren Richards," she said. They didn't shake hands. Loren had a supercilious little smile on his lips, but his eyes were as still and as steady as the eyes of a snake. She couldn't see Dan's eyes and Loren's were too fascinating to miss. But she felt the lack of friendliness, and it made her uncomfortable. To cover the bad moment she began explaining, feeling as if she had explained it a dozen times already, "Mr. Richards is a writer looking for a story. And Mr. Pierce is an attorney and is in real estate too and has come to talk about selling this property."

Loren said to her, "I didn't know you were thinking of selling."

And the other man demanded, "What kind of writing?"

"Many kinds," Loren Richards answered.

"Are you with a newspaper?"

"No. No newspaper."

Jo thought that Dan was overdoing it a little, so she quickly edged in. "It's quite all right. He has my permission to look around."

The writer's dark eyes turned to her and seemed to give her a silent thanks. But the hand of the other man touched her waist and turned her back toward the house.

"If you'll excuse us, Richards...."

"Sure."

She had a feeling that he stood watching as they went back to the porch. But Dan Pierce was talking, demanding her attention.

"I think I can move it pretty fast, Jo, if you want me to. In the meantime I've got a beautiful house in town you'd like. You could move right in. In fact, I wish you would. This is an interesting place, but spooky as hell, you know?"

"A little spooky, maybe. But I don't want to sell it anyway, Mr. Pierce."

"Oh, come on now, call me Dan."

"All right. But didn't your father tell you I didn't want to sell the house?"

"Yes, but we both feel you should reconsider."

Jo shook her head. "No. Even if I didn't stay here, I don't think I'd ever sell it. After all, it was his home."

"You don't mind if I come back and try to talk you into changing your mind, do you?"

"You'd just be wasting your time."

"You don't want to see me again?"

He looked as if she had hurt his feelings, and she hurried to say, "Oh, of course. I didn't mean that."

"Look," he said. "I know you're not married and I want you to know I'm not. And I'd like to date you. Would you go out with me tonight? I'll take you back to civilization, and dinner and a dance. How about it?"

"Thank you, but I just couldn't."

"Why?"

"I couldn't leave Mrs. Alcorn here alone. You see this is our first night here, and she might feel nervous alone."

"We could take her along. She could go back to town for the night."

"No, please. Not tonight."

"Some other time then?"

"Yes."

He saluted casually and left, and with the sound of his car went almost all sound. Only the high moaning of the pines was left. Even though she knew what it was, still she shivered. Her eyes searched the deepening shadows around the carriage house for a while, but did not find the dark-clothed writer. He too must have gone, she decided, and felt as if a quality of excitement had gone out of her day. Slowly, she went into the house.

How different this night was from the other, Jo thought as she later watched Mrs. Alcorn knit. The housekeeper had chosen the leather chair beside the hearth and sunk into it as if it had long conformed to her. Across the hearth, where she faced the open hall door, Jo relaxed in one of the new comfortable chairs. It was big enough that she could curl her legs in beside her.

The hallway was softly lighted by small kerosene lamps in wall brackets, and looked so warm and friendly that Jo only vaguely remembered her fear of the night alone. Thank heaven she hadn't told Mrs. Alcorn.

The minutes dragged and she was surprised when the old clock struck seven. Only seven. She thought of Dan Pierce's offer and wished she had gone. But of course there was Mrs. Alcorn.

Breaking into the softness of knitting needles and slowly ticking clock, she asked, "Mrs. Alcorn, would it bother you to stay here alone for a few hours in the evening?"

"Not if I could get them doors locked good and tight. Any time you want to leave, you go right ahead. I'll be here when you get back."

"I just wondered because Dan Pierce asked me to go out with him."

"He comes from a good family. I worked for his mother. You could certainly do a lot worse. I'd watch out for that dark one though. I'd say he's more devil than man."

Jo didn't answer. Strange, she thought, that they should choose the same comparison.

Then Mrs. Alcorn said, "Not that that's much worse, though. I'd about as soon tangle with the Devil as a man."

Jo laughed merrily, remembering a few men of her own she'd felt the same about. "Mrs. Alcorn, you were married, weren't you?" She meant it as a joke, but Mrs. Alcorn snapped the answer at her.

"Yes, of course I was."

Jo decided Mrs. Alcorn was just like Dunrope, suspicious until convinced otherwise. She got up, stretched, and got a book down from the shelf. It was an old work of fiction, the pages yellowed and crisp.

"Good night, Mrs. Alcorn. I think I'll read in bed awhile."

Mrs. Alcorn lay aside her knitting. "Let me get you a lamp."

In a moment she was back from the kitchen, a kerosene lamp in her hand. "Now when you're ready to go to sleep just blow in the top of the globe. And if you want to turn it down and leave a night light just twist this little wheel."

"Thank you."

Jo went upstairs and into the first room on the left, a room that obviously had been that of a girl. She pulled the shades against the dark night and put the lamp on a bedside table. By the light of the lamp she settled down in bed to look through the book. She tried to read, but found the prose long-winded and dull and could not concentrate enough to become interested. She finally lay the book aside, blew out her lamp, and lay looking into the dimly lighted hall.

There were two small round wall brackets at the bottom of the stairs, two at the top, all out of her sight, and two more at the end of the wide upstairs hall in view of her bed, and in all of them Mrs. Alcorn had placed small lamps that would burn low all night. For the first time Jo's attention became fixed on the small door that was situated between the two little lamps at the end of the hall. She had seen it before, of course, but for some reason had passed it by. Suddenly with a flash of visualization she remembered the exterior of the house, its height and the large hip roof that covered it. Above the second-story windows the height of the third story rose with only one tiny window at the back. The attic. And she had completely forgotten it.

She slipped out of bed and padded barefoot to the little door, wondering as she went if the painters had overlooked the attic too. She recalled that Mr. Pierce had said the personal belongings of the Stark family had been packed away. Why hadn't she thought of the attic? In the excitement of having the house redone she had completely forgotten that the answer to her questions about her father's family could probably be found in the attic. But the door was probably locked, and there was nothing to do but wait until morning to open it. Even if it weren't locked...

She stood within reach of the small knob, gazing at it, feeling a sudden unwillingness to touch it. Chills moved down her arms, pricking warningly, and she turned and ran back to bed, feeling every step of the way that someone was right behind her.

She snuggled down into the bed and faced the door again, calling herself a silly, nervous idiot. She tried to sleep, but sleep eluded her as questions began pouring into her mind. Why had her father been left at an orphanage at the age of fourteen months? If the elderly Stark had thought enough of the child to leave him all his wealth, then why had he allowed that child to be given into the hands of others to start with? And why had he not tried to find him in the years between the child's birth in 1900 and his own death in 1952? What had caused the death of the one girl, and what had happened to the other? Who had died, her father's mother or his aunt? And wasn't it odd that she, a twenty-two-year-old girl, had finally been brought home? All at once she understood the writer's interest in the story. There were too many unanswered questions, too many possibilities. Well, he was the story hunter, not she.

She awoke to the songs of birds in the pine boughs outside her window. The shades were up. . . the hall lights out. Mrs. Alcorn evidently had already come upstairs and gone down again.

Jo got up, dressed in pants and loose shirt, combed her brown hair into a straight fall, and went downstairs. She sat at the table in the kitchen, ate toast and drank a glass of milk, and assured Mrs. Alcorn she wouldn't die of malnutrition because she refused to eat eggs and cereal.

She was standing out under a tall pine looking up at the box-like top of the house when a staccato voice behind her said, "Good morning."

She nearly lost her breath in her sudden fright, and turned to see with scarcely any relief that it was Loren Richards.

"Say," he laughed, and the laughter was soft, a surprising difference. "I seem to be scaring you a lot, and I apologize again. Are you extraordinarily nervous or am I an especially frightful person?"

She relaxed into a smile. Today he was dressed in a yellow shirt, rolled high on his muscular arms, and looked especially handsome. "It's neither you nor me, I think," she said. "It's this setting and this house. For some reason I'm just not as comfortable here as I thought I would be. I'm determined to be comfortable though, because I like it, but—" As she talked she watched his eyes go serious, and she realized she was sounding far more serious than she had intended. Why was she telling this stranger her feelings?

"I think I understand what you feel," he said, when she hushed suddenly. "Some houses seem to have a kind of life of their own."

"Yes, I've heard that said before. Especially old houses where people have lived and died." She looked up again at the top of the house. "I was wondering about the third story. It seems to be as large as all the rest of the house, yet it must be just an attic, because there's only that one tiny window."

"Yes, I noticed that. You've not been up there?"

"No. Strangely enough, I didn't even think of it. You see, I spent the one night here alone and went right away the next morning and got a contractor to redo the bedrooms and part of the downstairs. I never even thought of an attic."

"What kind of entrance does it have? Does it have a stairway, or just a hole in the ceiling the way some old houses do?"

"There's a small door, and I guess stairs. I can see the door from my bedroom."

"Let's go up."

He sounded excited. Like a little boy with a treasure map. She looked at him for a moment, then decided, Why not?

They went around the house and in the front door, and she left it open to the heavy scent of pine and the still warmth of the sunny day.

When she saw him looking about she asked, "Do you want to see the rest of the house first?"

"Not really. It's lovely now, but I expect the attic to be more engrossing."

"Oh, that's right, you're story hunting. I was thinking of that last night, and began to see that it is a strange setup. I had been so dazzled and so preoccupied with other things that I never stopped to really wonder why Dad was put in that orphanage. But the more I think of it, the more I wonder why. I suppose that's what you want to know too?"

"Partly," he answered with the smile she was learning he used when he wanted not to answer a question or reveal his thoughts.

She ran up the stairs ahead of him, past the door to her room and two more bedroom doors, and stopped at the bend in the hall by the small attic door. She reached out to touch the knob, but drew her hand quickly back. She still didn't want to touch that knob. It was like a metal that repelled and she felt her fingers tingle. She rubbed them against the smooth material of her pants.

"You open it," she said, moving out of his way. Without hesitation he turned the knob, but the door didn't open. "Locked. Do you know where the key might be?"

"No." Then she remembered the drawer of keys and small tools in the kitchen. "But I might at that." She leaned over the banister and called, "Mrs. Alcorn, would you mind bringing the keys from that drawer up here so I can open the attic door?"

Mrs. Alcorn answered back, saying she would, and Loren said, "Is it all right if I peek into the bedrooms?"

She waited while he looked into each one, but he showed little interest. At her door he just glanced in, then looked at the attic door.

"This, I guess, is the room you chose. It's the only room from which the attic door would be visible from the bed."

"Yes, it is."

"Why did you choose it?"

"I don't know. I just liked it better. It was a girl's room, for one thing, and I thought maybe my grandmother's."

"There were two girls, weren't there?"

"Yes. How did you know?"

He smiled at her. Aha, she thought, he doesn't want me to know how he knows. But then he said, "I asked your Mr. Willis about the family. He told me all he knew, he said, but he didn't."

"He didn't?"

"No. I overheard what he told you—about the voice waking him. He didn't tell me that."

"Well, I suppose he felt you wouldn't understand. Anyway, that wasn't about the family."

"It was about the house and in its way about the family too."

"Don't you think he might have imagined it?"

"I don't know. What do you think?"

Mrs. Alcorn's appearance eliminated a need for an answer. She came heavily up the stairs, gave Loren a hard glare and Jo a handful of rusted keys. "Here they are. All I could find. What are you aiming to do?" She cast another dark glance at Loren Richards.

"We're going up into the attic if we can unlock the door."

"Well, maybe that old man would know where the key is. I don't know. If that door's never been opened I don't know if I'd want to go up there." Still, she stayed, her arms folded across the well-filled-out apron front, watching while Loren sorted through the keys and tried a couple that didn't fit. Finally, he chose one that he easily inserted but couldn't turn. He took a tighter grip on the key with his handkerchief and it slowly began to move. "There it goes," he said, and the door clicked open to reveal what at first seemed only to be a dark hole in the wall.

Jo and Mrs. Alcorn crowded close behind him to look into a narrow steep stairwell that was filled with cobwebs and darkness. The steps were several feet back from the door and seemed to have been built almost on top of each other.

"Whew!" spat Mrs. Alcorn. "Fit for a witch, nothing else. If the rest of the house looked like this—"

Loren was just standing there looking up, evidently speechless for once.

In a voice so low it was almost a whisper, Jo said, "Mr. Pierce said the Stark housekeeper packed some things away when Great-grand-father Stark died. I'll bet this door hasn't been opened since."

Loren asked, "Did you look in his desk?"

"Yes, and it was cleaned out."

"Then his papers, if any are left, are up here. I've noticed that housekeepers like to burn papers, though. Shall we go up and look?"

Jo hesitated just a moment. "We'll need a light."

"Have one right here," he said, taking from his pocket a small tube. "Little, but adequate."

He pointed it at the dark stairwell, and it was almost like a bright star in a dark sky. "Well," he said apologetically, "it makes more of a showing, usually."

"If you've got a match, here's a better light," Mrs. Alcorn said as she reached for the lamp in a wall bracket.

"I carry matches too," he answered, giving Jo a quick, boyish smile. "Just in case my trusty light fails completely."

Loren led the way up the stairs, with his tiny light that seemed to grow brighter each step, knocking cobwebs down with his hand as he went, and Mrs. Alcorn brought up the rear with her lamp. When they reached the top of the stairs and stood at last in the attic, it was like coming into a large cavern. Instead of partitions, carefully spaced supporting posts stood like black and silent monsters with their short cedar arms sticking out and in many cases holding limp old garments and rags. The one window was so small and so covered with dust and cobwebs it was hardly visible. Scattered about were the usual old relics and old furniture. The room really seemed more empty than Jo had expected. Loren was shining his small light on the rounded lid of a trunk. Then he swept the light across the floor, and Jo's eyes followed it, seeing an occasional box tied with a light rope, and another trunk.

The light swung back to the trunk by his feet, and he touched it with his toe. "This trunk isn't locked. See, the latch is open. Shall we look inside?"

"Yes, go ahead."

He squatted beside it and raised the lid and chuckled when it gave a long, loud squeak. "Doesn't like being bothered after all these years."

The trunk was full, and on top, wrapped in kitchen towels, were three framed photographs. Loren unwrapped them and placed them side by side so they all could see, and Mrs. Alcorn held the lamp close.

Two girls and one man. The man had a long, narrow, and very solemn face, thin hair parted in the middle. He could have been anywhere from thirty to fifty years old. The girls also wore center parts in their hair, but all resemblance ended there. One of them was dark and the other very fair and very blond. The face of the blond girl was exquisite, her lips curved and full, her eyes large and heavily lashed. She had been young at the time of the portrait. Perhaps as young as fifteen. The dark girl's face was a bit too round to be beautiful, her eyes pretty but not outstanding. Jo would have called her cute, but never beautiful.

She bent over Loren's shoulder. "I wonder if one of those was Dad's mother?"

"Evidently," he answered, as if his mind was occupied with a problem.

"Well," Jo said in an effort to lighten the gloom, "then I choose her," she pointed at the beauty, "and I hope I grow up to look just like her."

Loren Richards glanced up at her, amused, but Mrs. Alcorn said dourly, "She looks wicked to me."

"Why do you say that?" Loren probed, looking again at the picture, taking it up into his hands and turning it so that the light fell directly on it. And it was Jo's turn to feel amusement. He didn't know Dunrope or Mrs. Alcorn either. Naturally she would say that.

But Mrs. Alcorn set about pointing out reasons. "That face is too angelic. Look at them eyes. That girl had no conscience. Any time you see eyes that innocent, you can bet your life there's no heart there, no understanding of suffering or pain or wrongdoing."

Jo's amusement had vanished because suddenly it seemed Mrs. Alcorn was right.

Loren said, "You might have something there. Yes, I believe you might." He handed the photographs up to Jo. "Maybe you'd like these on your desk." Then he began unwrapping a large book. "Just as I hoped, the family Bible. Let's see here. . ."

Jo saw on the page of birth entries, written in a large flowery perfect penmanship, the names Elizabeth Jane, born October 15, 1880, and Marian Minerva, born October 15,1880.

She cried, "Twins? But they don't look anything at all alike! Aren't there any more names or information?" She saw the rest of the page bare, but asked anyway.

"Nothing," Loren said, turning pages. "Except this. A so-called Holy Union consummated on July twelfth, eighteen-seventy-six, between Benjamin Alden Stark and Melissa Maybelle Landers.

"Not even a death," Mrs. Alcorn murmured, as if to herself.

Loren said, "I don't think he kept very good record of births and deaths. At least not here."

"No," Jo said. "My dad isn't even. . . " Suddenly she recalled something. "Mr. Pierce said dad's name was given as David Stark. He — why—he must have been illegitimate!"

"Does that bother you?" Loren asked.

"Uh—gosh, I don't know. I guess not. It's just that I hadn't thought of it before."

"What I can't understand," Mrs. Alcorn said, "was why didn't he record the deaths? Not even his wife is mentioned again. I wonder why he never mentioned his wife again?"

Jo hardly heard her. An unaccountable sense of sadness had entered her like an invisible alien being. "I don't even know my dad's birthday. And, I don't know which one is my grandmother, or anything."

Loren stood up and brushed his trouser legs. "Why don't we go out where we can breathe? It's stuffy in here. I'll check through it later if you want me to. Or maybe I should say if you'll let me."

Jo didn't answer him. A terrible mental depression made her feel like sinking down and staying there. Only his hand on her arm helped her toward the light of the stairwell.

They left Mrs. Alcorn in the kitchen and went out into the sunshine, out of the pines behind the house, near the edge of the cliff. But Jo couldn't keep her gaze from going to the solid wall of the dark attic, broken on this side by the ridiculously small window. It looked like a single eye, glaring down at them. She shivered in the warmth of the sun and forced herself to look away. It was something like waking from a bad dream to find everything is at least normal.

"Loren, what do you think of a girl almost twenty-three, who's supported herself and lived alone for five years, suddenly becoming a coward?"

"What are you afraid of?"

"I don't know."

"Did the attic scare you?"

"Well, no, I think it was the picture of that girl. That may sound dumb, but—"

"No, it doesn't sound dumb. It was probably a combination of everything, including what Mrs. Alcorn said."

She drew a deep breath. "Maybe. But I think I'll stay out of the attic from now on. And I think I'll send the photographs back up to the trunk." When he didn't reply, she looked up to see that he was staring up at the tiny window, and there was something in his face, an alertness, that made her ask quickly, "What is it?"

"See, the cobwebs are moving."

They were. Back and forth, brushing against the window as if a strong draft of wind blew them.

"We must have left the door open." Even as she said it she distinctly remembered seeing Loren shut the door. "Maybe Mrs. Alcorn went back up.

"Why would she do that? I'll go see."

She watched him go around toward the front door, and then she turned back toward the kitchen to see if Mrs. Alcorn was there. Not finding her, she went on into the library.

Mrs. Alcorn was just coming across the room. She stopped, as if

Jo had startled her. "I heard someone go up the stairs," she said, in a hushed voice. "And it was that writer again. Did you tell him he could go back up there?"

"Yes. He went to close the door." Why, she wondered, would Mrs. Alcorn want to go back into the attic?

"He already closed the door," Mrs. Alcorn said. "I was there when he done it and so was you. If you ask me he just wants to snoop around."

There would be no earthly reason why Mrs. Alcorn would want to go up into that dungeon, Jo thought. And with dismay realized the words her mind had chosen: "No *earthly* reason?"

Mrs. Alcorn stared at her. "What?"

Jo backed away, toward the door and the sunshine at the edge of the pines. "It's all right," she said, "if he goes up."

She had been so comfortable with Mrs. Alcorn, and suddenly now she wanted to get away from her.

The sun felt good on her face. She walked the few feet more to the edge of the cliff and sat down, looking down into the valley, feeling the sun warm on her cold body. Her thoughts went back to the look on Mrs. Alcorn's face when she met her in the library. Surprise, yes. Guilt too? She had felt so safe with Mrs. Alcorn, but now she couldn't shed the feeling that Mrs. Alcorn had lied about the attic.

And she couldn't imagine why.

CHAPTER 4

She was still sitting there later, feeling lonely for Dunrope as if it were last year and she was going through his death again. She felt a need to put her arms around his fat neck and lay her cheek against his head as she had when she was a little girl and something went wrong, or when she was just feeling the need of companionship and someone to love. When she heard the footsteps behind her, she thought it was Loren Richards. But the voice that so cheerfully said, "Lovely day, right?" was not Loren's.

She looked up into Dan Pierce's smiling face.

He wasn't nearly so attractive as the writer, but he was more cheerful and far less serious, and all at once she felt glad that he had come.

"Right," she said, and patted the ground beside her. "Have a seat, Mr. Pierce."

"Ah, you make me feel old when you call me that, and I refuse to sit on damp ground, even by you." His hand reached for hers and he pulled her up. "And I don't want you sitting there either. You worry me, did you know that?"

"No, I didn't know." But she was glad someone worried about her. "How do I worry you?"

"By sitting too close to the edge of the cliff and on damp ground, and by being stubborn and living off out here in the sticks by yourself."

His hand on hers felt big and strong and warm. "I'm not by myself," she said.

"Practically. I came out to get you."

"To get me?"

"Yes. I want to show you some houses and take you to lunch and, well, just be with you."

"All right. Let me tell Mrs. Alcorn I won't be home for lunch."

"Tell her you may not be back at all. I may just keep you."

Even if he was joking, it was fun, she thought. Fun to be flirted with and treated as a desirable woman. "What's this?" she said. "Your prelude to talking a girl into selling the roof over her head?"

"I was serious," he answered, and he almost looked as if he might be.

She pulled her hand out of his and ran. "I'll be back in a moment."

A small purse with a few dollars, a comb and lipstick and a couple of tissues were in the desk drawer in the library. She got it, and went through into the kitchen. Mrs. Alcorn was sitting on a stool, peeling apples.

"I won't be here for lunch, Mrs. Alcorn. I'm going to town with Dan Pierce."

"All right. Be careful though. The highways are dangerous these days."

"Mrs. Alcorn, you don't have to do much cooking for me. I don't eat much."

The apple fell from Mrs. Alcorn's hand, and the paring knife drooped. She didn't look up. "I thought you might like an apple pie."

Jo felt that she had hurt Mrs. Alcorn's feelings, and she was sorry she had said anything. She touched the housekeeper lightly on the shoulder. "I would. I really would. I just don't want you to do more than you need to."

Mrs. Alcorn picked up the apple again. "Don't fret about me. I won't hurt myself."

That was better, Jo thought. The moment was gone. She recalled the feeling of distrust she'd had earlier and regretted that too. She was sure it had to do with her own mental depression. One thing about Dan—he had dispelled it entirely. An afterthought turned her back to Mrs. Alcorn. "If you need to go to town for anything, Mrs. Alcorn, feel free to take the car. I don't mind."

"I don't drive."

"Oh. Well. Any time you want to go just say so. I'll drive you."

"I don't need to go anywhere. Go along and have a good time."

The ride to town lightened Jo's feelings even more. Dan showed her a couple of houses she thought it might be nice to have, but when she thought of selling her great-grandfather's house, she couldn't say yes.

"You don't have to sell the other place," he said, drawing her to him, his arms loosely around her waist, yet holding her away so that he could look down at her. She didn't resist his casual embrace. There was always the curiosity about how a man's kiss would feel, always the search for the one kiss that would set her world afire. They were alone in the vacant house, in a room that was drawn and dim. "Jo, little Jo. Do you believe in love at first sight?"

His eyes weren't really blue, she was thinking, they were gray with blue specks, like blue-coated pottery that had at one time been shattered.

"Do you?" he asked again.

"No."

His arms pulled her tight against him and his lips brushed hers, playing gently. "I was hoping you'd say yes. But I didn't either until yesterday. Do you know why I changed my opinion on that yesterday,

Jo?" He kissed her firmly, not giving her a chance to answer his question. "Because of you," he said when the kiss ended. "When I saw you, I knew there is such a thing as love at first sight, and I was sorry I hadn't gone to see you sooner. My dad kept after me. Said he didn't want you to live up there alone. I said why not? Now I know why not."

She waited, and when he didn't go on and say why she asked, "Why, then?"

"Because I'm afraid something terrible will happen to you and I'll lose you without ever having you."

She laughed. "But what could happen to me?"

"I don't know. But I wonder about something. How much do you know about that man who says he's a writer?"

"Nothing, but—"

"I think I'll check him out. I don't like him. You may think I'm just being jealous, and I may be, but I've got a feeling he's not safe to have around. Anyway, I don't want him around you." He kissed her again, a longer kiss that came close to being the most possessive kiss she'd ever had. But she might as well have been made of wood. "Why don't you tell him to stay away?" he asked. "Want me to tell him?"

She twisted out of his arms. "No, please. He isn't bothering me. Why on earth would he want to hurt me?"

"I don't know the answer to that, but I'm going to find out if he's a writer or not, and where he's from."

They went from that house to lunch, and after lunch he drove to another house in the residential area where big houses were surrounded by big well-cared-for lawns.

"Another house for sale?" she asked.

"No, this is my home. I don't live here now. I have an apartment in town. I just wanted to show you to my mom."

"Oh, no, please! Not while I'm dressed like this."

"You're darling like that."

"No. Some other time, okay? I'm tired anyway, I should go home now."

He drove slowly on by the house. "Whatever you want. But you will let me bring you here for dinner soon, won't you?"

"Yes."

When they reached the log house, dark under the pines, and he parked in the driveway at the front veranda, he kissed her again. But this time she felt herself instinctively stiffen and draw away.

"Why did you do that?" he whispered. 'What's wrong?"

She glanced toward the house. There was not a movement anywhere. It might have been totally deserted. But she couldn't tell him that suddenly his lips had seemed repulsive, so she said, "Someone might be looking."

"So what? I'll tell anyone who's interested that I'm in love with you." He looked beyond her, though, at the dark reflection of the shadowed windows. "But I don't see anyone. In fact it looks dead here. Jo, can I come in with you? I hate even to leave you here."

"But, Dan, this is my home, and Mrs. Alcorn is here."

"Are you sure?" He opened the car door suddenly and got out. "I'm not moving away from here until I see for myself. I know she's okay. I'll leave you in her care, but I won't leave you alone."

Jo quietly followed him, not sure how she felt about so much solicitude. She guessed she had been on her own too long really to like it.

For a moment when they first entered the front hall it seemed the house was deserted and Mrs. Alcorn gone. But then came the smell of apple pie and a dull *bang* as the big oven door was closed.

"She's here, see?" Jo said, smiling at Dan. She didn't want to invite him in. She had been in his company for hours and felt the need to be alone. "So it's safe after all."

"All right, I'll leave you. But reluctantly."

She let him kiss her goodbye, then closed the door behind him, and locked it. She watched through the tiny glass slit as he drove away. When the car was gone, she went on into the kitchen.

The room was warm and fairly cheerful, considering how dark it was.

"Hello, Mrs. Alcorn. The pie smells delicious." A glance out the back window showed her that the sun had gone behind a cloud, and the sky was more cloudy than clear now.

"Well, when did you get back?"

"Just now."

"I didn't hear the car."

"The tires were very quiet on the drive. Something about the pine needles, I guess."

"You didn't see that writer yet, then?"

"No. Why?"

"Well, not long after you left he came downstairs and asked where you had gone. He said he'd like to go back up, so I told him you'd said he could. Then he messed around up there for a long time and came down wanting to know when you'd be back. I told him I didn't know. Later he came asking again. Finally he told me he'd found something and wanted to see you. So I thought maybe you'd seen him."

"What did he find?"

"I don't know. He didn't tell me that."

"Where is he now? Upstairs?"

"No, he ain't up there. He went on out. I saw him looking down over the cliff once. And another time I saw him out by the garage—or whatever that is."

The alarm clock on the table indicated the time to be almost four. Enough time before dark to see if she could find out what Loren Richards had wanted.

She went directly to the carriage house and entered, calling out, "Anyone here?"

Only the small animal in the wall answered her, moving quickly, then falling still as if it had stopped to listen. She looked inside, finding it very gloomy and dark, and filled with invisible eyes. She backed out and closed the door, leaving the small one his silence and his darkness.

The pine woods seemed unusually dim and shadowed this afternoon, and the air hung so still there was no singing in the treetops. She looked toward the house, then turned her back to it and wondered where the path was he'd said lay beyond the cliff. She had no doubt he had gone home. Home to his camp—whatever that might be—down on the river. She was as anxious to see him as he was to see her. She wanted to know what he had found, so she began the search for the path.

There seemed to be nothing but pine needles, but as she neared the slope of the hill and the cliff dwindled to a few large boulders, the pine forest dwindled too, giving way to underbrush and tall maple and oak trees. And finally she found the faint narrow trail down the hillside.

It had probably been a deer path to start with, but it led directly down to the river as if two young girls at one time had used it to reach their private swimming beach.

The water moved rapidly along at this narrowed point, sweeping at the muddied bank beneath the path. Farther upstream, she could see, the river widened, and there was the smooth naked surface of the beach. A long streak of lightning passed through the clouds overhead and ended with a loud *crack* as if a great hand had snapped a rope of fire. The rain started at the same time, sprinkles, large and cold, that felt heavy as hailstones.

She hurried toward the gravel bar ahead where the river lay wide and calm, where she hoped to find a tent. How else would a man be camped?

She rounded the last part of the hill and saw the open space in full, and saw the gravel and sand clean and bare as if no one had ever set foot there. She stopped, mildly surprised, disturbingly puzzled. The rain grew heavier, wetting her hair and clothes.

To the left was the road, curving down close to the river then pulling away again into the great backwoods beyond. And she stood alone where Loren Richards had said he was camped.

He had lied to her then.

Overhead the storm had grown to a screaming fire-streaked fury, and she turned running toward the path. She hadn't realized it was so close to the water in places. The rain made the path slippery, and she was forced to move cautiously, her hands grasping the weeds and underbrush on one side to keep her from falling into the muddy roar of the river on the other side. And darkness came down, early and quickly so that her way was lit only by the lightning.

Finally she was away from the river and climbing the hill into the pine forest, but one fear had simply been replaced by another, for now the lightning scarcely penetrated the thick cover of pines and the path was gone. There too was the high moan and cry in the trees as the storm's wind tore at them.

She had nothing to guide her here until her hands touched a pile of stone and she guessed it to be the other end of the rock wall. She fought her way along it, hoping the vines that so often tripped her were not poison ivy, and finally she came to the end of the wall. This meant a gate, and a road, and if she turned left—the house.

The tiny light through the trees was the most welcome thing she had ever seen. Nearly sobbing in relief she ran toward it. A light in a window of a house—any house.

Mrs. Alcorn stood in the open door as if she had been watching a long time. "My Lord'a mercy," she said as Jo ran in under the protection of the porch. "Where have you been, girl?" She got Jo by the arm, pulled her into the warm library and over to the hearth. "You wait there while I get some towels. I'll fix you a hot bath and get your pajamas and robe. If you don't die of pneumonia, I'll be surprised. Where have you been so long?" She sounded as furious as the storm, but her voice faded as she went toward the bathroom for towels.

When she returned Jo explained, "I went down to the river and got lost."

"My Lord'a mercy. I didn't know where you'd gone. Out in a storm like this!"

The first sneeze didn't come until she'd had her bath and was on her way to the chair by the hearth, and she was glad of that because Mrs. Alcorn immediately brought out a blanket and tucked her into the chair, and then brought some horrible concoction she called medicine.

Jo frowned into the smelly slimy stuff and asked, "What on earth *kind* of medicine?"

"Never you mind. It's my own mother's recipe, and it's guaranteed to keep you from getting pneumonia. Drink!"

Jo drank it and then shuddered and gagged and shrank into her blanket hoping she'd never have to drink another glass as long as she lived. Mrs. Alcorn grunted in glum satisfaction and took the glass back to the kitchen. When she came back she had a basket of knitting, and she settled down in her chair across from Jo.

"Relax, now, and rest," Mrs. Alcorn ordered. 'When you're ready to go upstairs, you'll find your bed warm. I put a hot water bottle in it. Too bad there's no electricity. If ever a house needed electric blankets on the beds, this one does."

Jo didn't answer. She felt drowsy and warm, and so glad to be home. She watched the knitting needles flash in the firelight and heard the lazy tick of the clock under the noise of the unrelenting storm.

The whole of the house was restfully dim and the fire alternately lightened and shadowed the area within its reach. It had a hypnotic effect. Jo felt the waves of approaching sleep move through her brain in long slow rhythms that came closer and closer together. Part of her mind seemed still alert and part had already succumbed. It was as though one part of her brain stood unresistingly and watched another part draw it under into the world of sleep and dreams.

Suddenly her consciousness leaped forward, as if an outside force had tapped her on the forehead, and the sleep waves receded. Her eyes were closed, yet she was sharply aware of her surroundings. Mrs. Alcorn sat in front of her, knitting. And beyond Mrs. Alcorn, in plain view, was the open hallway door, and the bottom of the stairs, and the round knob on the newel post....

Her eyes opened instantly to the newel post and saw there, lying limply on the round top, a very pale hand.

Someone was standing on the stairs.

Jo stared at the hand, terror paralyzing her throat. She wanted to cry out to Mrs. Alcorn to look behind her. My God, Look, stop knitting and look! But she was incapable of it. Helpless, curled under the blanket in her chair, she watched as the hand left the post and became part of a tall young woman. She walked past the door, a long white robe covering her feet and making her look as if she floated, her long silver-blond hair falling down her back.

Mrs. Alcorn suddenly got to her feet, her knitting rolling to the floor, her hands reaching for Jo's shoulders.

Jo shrank back, her eyes leaving the hall and focusing on the face that was coming down above her. And at last her throat ceased to be paralyzed and she screamed.

"You! Wake up! My Lord 'a mercy, wake up!" Mrs. Alcorn cried.

Jo stared up into the face and saw that there was no evil there, as it had seemed, only a startled expression of concern. Jo reached out and pushed Mrs. Alcorn to one side so that she could see into the hallway, but the girl was gone. She pointed a hand that shook uncontrollably.

"There was someone there!"

Mrs. Alcorn turned, looking toward the hall. But she didn't move. "Who was it?" she asked, not doubting. "Was it that writer?"

"No. It was a girl."

Mrs. Alcorn's face swung slowly back and she looked for a long moment at Jo. Then in a voice nearing normal she said, "Why, child, you had a nightmare."

"No! I wasn't asleep."

"Then you've got a fever. I thought at the start you were having a nightmare from the way you carried on, groaning, trying to cry."

"I wasn't asleep," Jo insisted, pressing her hand to her forehead. "I saw her as plainly as I see you. She came down the stairs and went out the front door, I think. You got in the way and I didn't see where she went."

Mrs. Alcorn's face sagged slightly, as if several emotions had passed through her, fear among them. "I reckon it could be possible," she said, and her voice was low. "A body could hide up in that attic and—that writer, he might have something to do with it. What did she look like?"

"She was very white, straight and quite tall, and she wore something white and sweeping, like a robe. And her hair was long and hung past her hips and was a beautiful silver-blond, like the hair of a Christmas angel. . . " Even as she described her Jo saw Mrs. Alcorn's face change again, withdrawing from her, and she knew why. Jo leaned forward, whispering sharply, "It was she, wasn't it? The girl in the picture! The one who lived here seventy-two years ago."

After a slight hesitation Mrs. Alcorn's hand reached out and touched her forehead. "And I know for sure now you've got fever."

Jo leaned her head back, sighing, relieved. Fever was better than such terrible fear. "Yes, I must have. I remember when I was small I had a fever and I thought I saw my mother. And she'd been dead almost a year. I certainly don't believe in ghosts. I guess she's been in my mind more than I realized. The girl, I mean."

"I think I'll put you to bed."

Jo smiled a little. "I think I'm ready to go."

In the warm blankets in her bed Jo felt more comfortable than she had downstairs, but she wished she dared give in to her uneasiness and call Mrs. Alcorn back to sit with her until she fell asleep. But that was silly. Let Mrs. Alcorn rest.

She turned over and wriggled deeper into the blankets. The beat of the rain against the window kept her company. Her room was in shadows, the lamp unlighted, and the little lamps in the hallway were turned so low that the attic door looked like a dark hole.

She raised up on an elbow and stared at it, and she began to see why the attic door was so dark, for it stood open, turned back against the wall, and it was the black interior of the stairwell that she saw.

The terror was in her again, and she couldn't rationalize it away. She considered calling out to Mrs. Alcorn to please come and close the attic door, but an instinct deep inside begged for silence, to lie down again in her bed and not breathe or move or otherwise attract attention to herself.

She lay staring at the open door, afraid to breathe, afraid to close her eyes, and knew she'd not be able to sleep. The door had to be shut —or her own door. She hadn't thought of her own bedroom door, and she slipped quickly out of bed and ran across the soft carpet and closed the door and leaned against it. Even in the now total dark of her room she felt safer, able to breathe. The lightning touched her window blind then and turned it on, like a flickering neon light, for a long moment. But she didn't let the blind up, and she didn't light her lamp. This time the darkness seemed a comfort. She ran back to bed and pulled the blankets in around her body and even over her head.

She slept and woke, and slept again, and dreamed of two girls, one fair and one dark, standing in the hall facing each other, and there was a feeling of terrible hatred. Then she heard the baby cry, in the room down the hall.

She pulled the covers back from her head to force away the fevered dream, and still the baby cried, gasping, gasping, like a small helpless animal searching for life.

The storm had gone. The room was black, without even the lightning outlining her window, and because she felt so helpless too and so afraid, and so very, very sad, she closed her eyes tight and wept into her pillow.

And still the baby cried.

CHAPTER 5

The next time Jo woke the room was light, her blind was up, the door open. And one quick glance showed her the attic door had been closed. Mrs. Alcorn had attended to all of it, of course, and let her sleep. But she felt as if she had not been asleep, as if she had spent the night in another world, a world that drained her of her life, her energy, her personality.

She was thankful that the baby had hushed, abruptly, and she had been able to sleep again. But she would never forget the sound. Never. It had scarcely seemed human at all. If Tom Willis hadn't told her it was a baby, she might not even have known.

She got her robe from the foot of the bed, but instead of going downstairs, she went slowly to the room down the hall and stood on the threshold looking in. She saw a blue shag rug, a blue-and-lavender-plaid bedspread and matching draperies on the window that looked out into green boughs. The room was cold, still, and empty. The furniture didn't change it, nor the carpet. This morning it was lifeless and cold. But last night a baby had been in this room. Or the echo of a baby—a baby who had lived there seventy-two years ago? Her dad? Had he come back again? Somehow come home?

She backed out of the room, put her hands on her head and squeezed it as if such a feeble motion could clear her brain of its fever and its silly waking dreams and imaginations. She had to tell herself that no matter how awake she felt, she wasn't awake at all.

She went downstairs and sat at the kitchen table, after a brief clean-up job in the bathroom, and drank a cup of hot coffee. Mrs. Alcorn lay a plump hand on her forehead again and pronounced her saved by the medicine.

"No fever this morning. You feel as cold as a snake."

"Well, thinks for the analogy," Jo said dryly, adding, "But I don't feel so well."

"No wonder. You just battled out a fever. But you'll be all right now if you'll be careful and not get chilled again. It's impossible to keep this house warm. And I'm going to tell that writer when I see him that I'd appreciate it if he'd shut that door up there after this, good enough that it'll stay shut!"

"You found it open this morning, I gather."

"Yes, I found it open, and I'm getting tired of finding it open. There he is now." She was already on her way to the door when he knocked.

He came in smiling, yet efficient and businesslike. His eyes found Jo and the smile almost disappeared. "'You're not feeling well?"

"No, she's not," Mrs. Alcorn snapped, "thanks to you."

His eyebrows lifted and he pointed a long finger at his chest. "Me! What did I do?"

"She went looking for you and got caught in the storm."

"Oh, say, I'm sorry. Really I am."

Jo looked up into his eyes, searching for the truth. "You said you were camped by the river. I believed you."

"But I went to town yesterday afternoon and didn't come back until just now. I *am* sorry, Miss Stark. If I'd known you'd be coming down yesterday evening, I wouldn't have gone at all."

"I didn't see any signs of someone camping there."

He gazed at her almost blankly a moment, the smile entirely gone. Then suddenly it returned. "Oh, you think I lied. I can see you don't rough it much. I drive a pickup camper."

The sudden happiness that filled her was almost startling. "I hadn't thought of that."

"Anyways," Mrs. Alcorn said, breaking into a moment from which she had been entirely omitted, "she nearly caught pneumonia, and I reckon it's not much of my business about whether or not you go upstairs, but after this I would appreciate it if you'd shut that attic door behind you, and lock it!"

He turned and gave his attention to Mrs. Alcorn. She had gone to the sink and was washing a dish she'd turned up somewhere, her back solidly toward him.

"You found it open again?"

"I did."

Jo saw his hand touch his chin in a gesture of thought. "I'm sorry. I'll be more careful." Then he turned and sat across the table from Jo, and took a letter from his pocket. "I found this yesterday. It was in the back of the Bible."

Jo looked at the creamy white envelope on the table, and reached for it slowly. She didn't anticipate what it could be, she only felt a reluctance to know, as if a protective curtain were suddenly to be drawn from her eyes.

"There's no name or address," she said.

"No. It was never mailed. You'll see it's good stationery. It's in very good shape. Actually, that's the reason I was gone so long. I went down to the university to have an old professor of mine check it out. I thought it might be a fake. But, Jo, it's not."

She took the pages from the envelope and spread them before her. The penmanship was large, perfect, and flowery, and she remembered seeing it before, in the Bible. The date on the letter was written July 3, 1900. And it was addressed to John Smith Sanitarium, to a

Dr. Rawlings. Jo moistened her lips, drew a deep breath, and began reading silently.

Dear Dr. Rawlings,

I cannot take the time to write in detail, as my need, once again, is so urgent. I feel I shouldn't even take time to enquire about my wife. I hardly have the time to wait for this letter to go, and for you to come. I live in terror of what my daughter will do. What you said could happen has happened, and I must get her out of the house and safely put away before she harms Marian. Yes, that sweet child we thought might help to keep Elizabeth sane is the one she has turned against the most. How I regret taking Marian as my own and teaching them they were sisters. But it can't be changed now, and I have no choice left but to put Elizabeth in the asylum too. How can a just God pass the seeds of insanity from mother to daugh

Jo looked up. "Is this all? Where's the rest of the letter?"

"That's it. You'll notice he stopped in the middle of the page. And I think if we'd check, we'd find the date on the gravestone out there is near the date on the letter."

Mrs. Alcorn, standing now behind Jo and reading over her shoulder, cried, "My Lord 'a mercy! He was too late, wasn't he? Do you think Elizabeth killed Marian?"

"I don't know." He pushed his chair back and stood up. "Shall we go see the grave? It's fairly warm out."

Jo wouldn't have cared if the temperature was zero. It didn't matter that she was still in her robe, she was already on her way. Mrs. Alcorn and Loren followed behind her.

The grave was enclosed in a rusted iron fence with spiked posts, in a lot about twenty feet square. Weeds grew almost as tall as the stone, as tall as the fence was high, and were now tangled and brown.

Underneath, as they pushed the brittle weeds away to make a path to the stone, they could see fine-leafed spring grass.

Jo stood before the stone with Mrs. Alcorn on one side of her and Loren on the other, and brushed her fingers across the name and the date: **MARIAN MINERVA STARK,** Oct. 15, 1880 - July 3, 1900.

A feeling of extreme sadness and depression moved through Jo like a swift dark undercurrent. "Yes," she said, "he was too late. I wonder how she died."

"Murder," Mrs. Alcorn said. "No doubt about that. Murdered by that crazy mean Elizabeth."

Jo moved back and looked around at the small enclosure that was so strikingly dominated by the stone in the center. "What a lonely place this is with the pines moaning overhead all the time. And how terrible that her grave should be so weedy. I'll have to ask Mr. Willis if he can clean it up.

Loren said, "I'll clean it."

Jo stopped on the outside of the fence and laid her hand on a rusted spike. A new thought suddenly entered her mind. "Then Marian wasn't his daughter. Perhaps she was the mother of the baby."

Mrs. Alcorn said quickly, "But they said the child was his *grandson.*"

Jo turned to Loren, a desperate move, as if he could save her. "But —isn't there a possibility that Marian was Dad's mother? If it really was Elizabeth then that means—I—" She swallowed, and moistened her dry lips. "I would prefer to think that Marian was my grand-mother. Isn't there some way I can find out? I must know!"

He stood beside her, looking down into her eyes. He seemed relaxed, leaning against the fence, but absent-minded and distant, as if he were thinking of something apart from her. "I'll find out if I can. Meantime, don't worry about it, that's two generations ago."

She shook her head, contradicting, remembering last night and putting a possibly different interpretation to it. "Oh, if only he had mentioned the baby! I wonder why he didn't mention the baby? Elizabeth, then—did she take the baby away? Or did he. . . ? No! They said his daughter ran away. She took the baby. Elizabeth, the insane Elizabeth took my father and left him—then he must have been her baby!"

Loren's hand gripped her shoulder as if he were going to shake her, but he didn't. "You're getting hysterical," he said calmly. "Watch it. Be careful. The power of suggestion is very strong."

"But don't you see?"

"No, I don't. Maybe she put the baby in the orphanage because he was not hers. Because he was Marian's, and she was jealous."

Mrs. Alcorn said, sounding very stubborn, "He called the boy his grandson."

Loren turned to Mrs. Alcorn. "I debated on not showing her that letter, and decided it was her property and not mine. I didn't think it would upset her this much. I wish you'd drop that grandson bit."

"Well, he said it, I didn't."

"Jo, listen," he said, ignoring Mrs. Alcorn. "You've been all right mentally all your life, haven't you? So why should you change all of a sudden? I'll go back upstairs and I'll dig the place apart and prove to you Elizabeth was not your grandmother."

He forcibly pulled her away from the grave and they went back toward the house. Jo heard Mrs. Alcorn speak softly, as if she were in the room of a sick patient. "She was seeing things last night already."

There was the slightest pause before Loren answered her, as though he considered not answering at all. "Like what?"

"I don't know. Ghosts. The girl in the picture."

"Jo, tell me about it, will you?"

But now she felt sentenced by it. It had all seemed real, but weren't all imaginings real to a sick mind? She didn't dare let it happen to her. "It was just a nightmare, I think."

They went on, silent. She was glad he didn't ask her again.

In the house they separated, Mrs. Alcorn stopped downstairs, Jo went to her room, and Loren on into the attic. As Jo dressed she could hear him walking above her, but it was not a comforting sound. She felt exposed, surrounded, as if she weren't alone in her room. As if someone stood behind her, silent and watchful. And full of hatred.

She turned quickly, the hairbrush falling from her hand, but there was no one there. Of course there was no one there. She bent to pick up the hairbrush, telling herself to stop being that way.

In the hallway she paused, looking at the open attic door and thinking of going up. But a cold draft swept her and she went down instead, seeking warmth. It was a cool day, cooler than Loren had suggested, and she had two choices, the big stove in the kitchen or the sun outside. The fireplace was cold, filled with the dead ashes of last night. Jo stopped by the hearth, thinking how she had always taken for granted heat that came from the touch of a thermostat.

Behind her Mrs. Alcorn's voice blared out unexpectedly. "I figured it would be like this when I saw that old man. No fire, no wood on time. If you ask me, he's probably dropped dead in his tracks and won't get no fire built today."

"If he doesn't come before long, I suppose we should go see about him."

Mrs. Alcorn grumped low in her throat. "That's about right. Us taking care of the caretaker! It wouldn't surprise me at all if we had to go build *him* a fire."

"I suppose," Jo said slowly, "it was foolish to try to live here. At least before summer comes. The house is too far back and too inconvenient. It won't take long to get ready to leave. We can simply cover the furniture."

"Leave? I can build a fire in the fireplace as well as I can in the stove, Miss Jo. That's no trouble. All I need is wood." Her tone had changed so abruptly that Jo looked around at her, puzzled. Mrs. Alcorn's eyes had grown large, like a child pleading. "Maybe you could get a local woodcutter to bring in a few ricks. That's all I need, just wood."

"You must have taken a liking to this place," Jo said.

Mrs. Alcorn nodded. "It'd be fairly peaceful here if that writer would stop prowling around and that old man would make up his mind to get some wood in. Besides. . ." she hesitated, and using the placating tone again, "I need the job." That was the first time Mrs. Alcorn had revealed a need. In the beginning, even the day Jo had met her, she had felt the lady was taking the job more as a favor to Mr. Pierce than anything else. In fact, hadn't she mentioned something about her social security?

"I thought you were already drawing social security, though I know that isn't much either."

"No. None," Mrs. Alcorn said. "I'm just fifty-nine. I have to support myself."

Footsteps clomping on the porch were followed by the door opening and admitting elderly Tom Willis looking ten years younger than he claimed to be. His ribbon arms strained under a load of wood.

"A mite late, ain't I?" he said cheerfully, dumping the logs onto the hearth. "It won't take long to get a fire goin' here."

Mrs. Alcorn snorted faintly and disappeared toward the kitchen, and Mr. Willis set about making conversation.

"Nice morning. A bit cool, but nice. Not a cloud in the sky, but we shore had us a storm last night, didn't we?"

"Yes."

"I couldn't help wondering about that Loren Richards, parked right on the river the way he was. I went down to see if he come through all right, and he was gone! That's why I was late with the far, here. Looked along the river a ways, then decided I'd better get on up here. Shorely he didn't get warshed away, I thought. Shore enough he didn't. There was his rig parked out front of the house here."

Jo moved to the window and looked out. She saw a yellow pickup camper, looking as bright and beautiful as a wild canary in a dark forest. Just seeing it made her feel more normal, as if she were in a familiar place again.

She smiled. "I didn't know it was parked there."

"You mean you ain't seen him? Well, I wonder where he could be?"

She came back from the window. "Oh, he's here. He's upstairs. In the attic. I just didn't know about the truck."

Tom Willis looked at the ceiling, as if he could see straight on up into the attic. "What's he doing up there?"

"Just looking around."

"Oh." Tom built the fire for a moment, carefully placing wood on the irons. He straightened, standing, and brushed his hands on his overalls. "I'll have to get some kindling now. You'd better be sure he locks that attic door when he comes down."

Jo was instantly alert. "Why?"

"Because it won't stay shut if it's not locked. The wall's a little crooked there I reckon, or the latch don't fit right. Makes the door swing back against the wall. Mr. Stark always kept it locked."

Jo was so relieved that she giggled. "And I thought it was haunted."

Tom Willis looked up through the ceiling again, and he didn't smile. "Well—I'd make sure it was locked, I'se you."

Jo felt like a child who has been scolded for being flippant in a serious situation, then she recalled that Tom Willis was as cowardly as she, and she forgave him. Seriously, she said, "I'll make sure."

He nodded, satisfied. And went out after the kindling.

Jo stood for a while in front of the fire after Tom had finished with it and gone on about his own business, but though it was warm it didn't satisfy her need this morning for sunshine. She wished that the trees didn't crowd so close to the front, keeping all morning sun away.

She got her sweater off the chair where she had dropped it, and put it on and went out. The sun filled the valley below, and had crept a few feet into her back yard. She sat down on a patch of moss that had turned warm under the sun. The day was still, and it was easy to relax. She watched the cattle for a while, looked at the view of mountains and sky, and then sat with her eyes closed, her mind tuned in only to nature, the feel of the sun, the high keen smell of pine-scented air. Did she really want to go back to a noisy city that smelled, as on her old street, of exhaust fumes and factory smoke?

She heard the door close, and the footsteps approach her. She looked up to see Loren, but she didn't move. He sat down beside her.

"You found nothing," she said. "I can see it in your face."

"Nothing conclusive. One of those trunks holds his wife's things, I believe. There's nothing much but clothes, rotten lace. But there was another picture."

"Of his wife?"

"I'm sure it is because she looks so much like Elizabeth."

Jo stared at him as if it would help assimilate something in the back of her mind. "How do you know what Elizabeth looked like? We saw two pictures. We didn't know which was Elizabeth."

"We do now," he answered. "Elizabeth was his wife's child, and the other, older picture looks like the blond girl. She's not as pretty, but there's no mistaking the eyes and the hair. So, we now know that the girl out there"—he nodded toward the grave,—"is the dark-haired girl. The adopted Marian. Poor kid, didn't know what she was in for, did she?"

"But we still don't know that the baby was hers." What was he trying to do—sentence her to a life of fear? Fear of her own mind. Impulsively, her hand went to her hair. "My hair is brown, it's not blond."

He smiled at her. "Right. And your eyes are brown, and your lashes are about an inch long and make you look very sweet and inno-cent. And your lips are luscious without lipstick and your skin is perfect and needs no makeup. But are you sure you don't look like your mother's people? What color was your dad's hair?"

She laughed, a natural response to his back-handed compliments. For a moment she forgot the other. "For crying out loud, what a letdown! You had me thinking you were going to tell me you'd fallen madly in love with my fantastic beauty, and then you want to know what color my dad's hair was!" Suddenly a picture of her dad was in her mind. Not the gray-haired father she had known, but earlier snapshots. The moment of lightness was gone, and she gazed across the valley and bit her lip.

"Well?" he urged.

"You're right," she said. "It was blond too. It looked almost white in the old snapshots. I still have them you know, stored away until I go back after them." She tried to laugh again but it failed and came out sounding like one of Mrs. Alcorn's snorts. "Isn't this something? I inherit wealth and insanity. Probably I'm raving mad and this is all in my mind. None of this is really happening."

"I give you my word it is happening. It's in my mind too."

She glanced impishly at him. "But what makes you think you count? You're only a figment of my mad imagination."

He reached for her, his arm sliding in under her bent knees. "In that case. . ." He pulled her onto his lap and kissed her. When he raised his face away she felt as if he drew all her strength. She trembled weakly. He smiled down at her, the laughter of male conquest in his eyes.

She gasped for breath and managed to sit up and push away from him. "I was all wrong," she murmured. "I'm a figment of *your* imagination."

He got lightly to his feet and pulled her up. She thought they were going to walk, but instead he turned her body toward his, to fit into the curve of his, and began kissing her again. She collapsed against him, her arms closing around him, straining him to her. For the first time in her life she belonged totally to a man, scarcely more than an extension of his body with no desire beyond being a complete part of him. Right in plain view of Mrs. Alcorn's kitchen windows.

She struggled. He didn't let her go, but the kisses ended. He was no longer laughing. His voice was low and breathless.

"Don't. Let me hold you. Remember, you're only a figment of my imagination, and I'm imagining you completely in my power and unresisting."

She gave a superhuman shove and got away. Then they smiled at each other, and she saw the difference in his smile. He had come forth, human, vulnerable. She saw in his eyes, and in the tenderness of his smile, that he was in love with her, and suddenly she wanted more than anything in the world just to hold his hand.

She clasped it in both of hers, and pressed it close to her body. She leaned her head against his shoulder and whispered under her breath, "I love you."

He didn't answer. Only his hand tightened on hers so that her own hand began to ache. He held it that way only a moment, then released it.

"Seriously now," he said, "isn't it worth it? I mean you've got what most people would give anything for. Wealth."

Her heart heard only two words—*seriously now*. When she looked up into his eyes she wondered how she could have thought him in love and vulnerable, capable of being hurt by her. His eyes seemed hard and darker, almost black, amused, probing, digging, and analyzing. What kind of man was he, after all? She had been serious, and he was saying he hadn't. Well, she'd not make a damned fool of herself again.

She tried to be gay. "Sure. I suppose if I had to, I could buy my own psychiatrist." She went toward the house at a brisk pace intended to get her away from him as fast as possible. She was not going to fall in love with a handsome demon of a man who couldn't care about anything but stories. She wasn't even going to talk to him anymore.

He kept pace with her, easily, at her side, as if he didn't know she was trying to run away from him. "Can you take knowing that Elizabeth was probably your father's mother?" he asked.

"Of course I can take it!" she snapped.

"Good, because if you can't—" he caught her arm and stopped

her at the edge of the porch. She was looking into his eyes again, as he demanded, and growing weak. But there was no weakness in his, "—you're in terrible danger."

He turned and was gone, around the corner of the porch to his pickup. The door slammed, the engine started, and a moment later she stood alone, looking at the driveway where he had been.

In the shade of the pines she grew cold again and she wished he hadn't left. Even though she didn't know what he wanted of her, anything was better than being so completely alone.

CHAPTER 6

Her longing for him beat continuously in her heart, her arms had need to hold him, her lips to kiss him. But he was gone now. There was only the sound of his truck fading on the road, and in a moment that too was gone. She put her arms around the post and leaned her cheek against it, feeling it cold and smooth.

Into her thoughts burst his last words then: Can you take knowing that Elizabeth was probably your father's mother? Good, because if you can't, you're in terrible danger.

Terrible danger. But why? That suggested more than just an old case of possibly inherited family insanity. She felt a growing anger. Why had he said that and then immediately gone away? The least he could have done was explain what he meant by it.

She was beginning to feel angry with everyone. Tom Willis for hearing things. Mrs. Alcorn for being such a grouch. Mr. Pierce for letting his son carry on a ridiculous search and finding her. And Loren Richards for kissing her. He had no damned business kissing her.

She went inside, slamming the door and feeling grumpily good about it. The letter was still on the kitchen table. She snatched it up and poked it into its envelope. "I won't be here for lunch, Mrs. Alcorn," she said, and went out to her car. She had a feeling Mr. Pierce knew more than he pretended. If he didn't, he was about to learn a few new facts. Terrible danger indeed.

Mr. Pierce was in, and came beaming to shake her hand. As soon as the door shut between them and his secretary, Jo gave him the letter.

"I insist on knowing about this," she said. "I'm tired of so much fog. I want to know absolutely which girl was my dad's mother. There must be a way to find out."

She watched Mr. Pierce's face carefully as he read the letter, but knew no more than she had to start. His pendulous jaws seemed to bounce a little, but that was all.

"I can't believe it," he said.

"Can't believe what?"

"This." He waved the letter. "I had no idea."

"And I can't believe it either," she said. "I can't believe there's no record of it."

"Where did you find it?"

"The letter? In the family Bible."

"Hmmm. I had no idea."

"You said that. I want it investigated. The whole thing. Check on Great-grandfather Stark's wife"—she paused, thinking, and added a bit less confidently,—"I guess that would be Great-grandmother Stark. Maybe. And I want to see the Stark will. I insist on seeing it." She was ready to fight for her right to see it, and was a little disappointed that Mr. Pierce gave in so quickly.

"Of course." He grunted to his feet and went through a door in the side wall. He closed the door tightly behind him and Jo was left in a room of total quiet. There was no noise from the street and no noise from the outer office. She thought it must be soundproofed, walls, ceiling, and floor. She waited.

The door opened again and Mr. Pierce came back through and

handed her several legal-looking pages. The more and farther she read, the more it seemed like a foreign language. Finally, trying not to appear too stupid and confused, she looked up. Mr. Pierce was leaning back in his chair as comfortable as a chunky frog on a lily pad, with just the merest of smiles on his lips.

"You will notice," he said, "that the family history is not explained at all. It states simply that all he possesses—and it's written out in detail to avoid misunderstandings—is to go to his grandson, David Stark, whose birthday was June second, nineteen-hundred. If the grandson is deceased, then it will go to his heirs, to be inherited and divided equally, but held in trust until each heir has reached the twenty-fifth birthday. If, after thirty years, David Stark or heirs are not found, the estate is to go to different charities, which are listed. You will notice also that not one word is said about his daughter or the girl who was not his daughter. David Stark is the only relative mentioned."

Jo placed the papers neatly on the desk in front of Mr. Pierce. She had to take his word for all he claimed was in the will. She began to feel beaten. "But isn't there some way we can find out? Check at that sanitarium, please. Check that doctor's records."

"We can do that. But after this long the records may have been destroyed. However, Miss Stark, we'll do as you wish. Glad to."

She knew she should go now, but she had a vague feeling that once she left the office, her chance would be gone. That here more than anywhere else, more than the Stark home or the sanitarium, was the answer she needed. Here, in this office, somewhere. Here.

"Where is your son's office?" she asked.

He nodded his head toward the room where he had gone. "There. I'm preparing to retire and Dan is taking over. In a few months we will be taking in my young nephew, then I'll go home to tend my roses. Dan isn't here at the moment, though. He spends most of his time at his real estate office."

She hadn't wanted to see Dan anyway. It had been an impulsive question. "Is this will all you have on the Starks?"

"All that is personal. Of course there is much more concerning the estate. But that's all business. Mostly dollars and cents. Of course, it's your property and you can look at it if you wish."

"No, I don't think so." She got up. There was no point in hanging around. "Thanks for your time, Mr. Pierce."

He was up and hurrying to get to the door ahead of her. "Come in any time you feel like talking, Miss Stark. We're always glad to see you." He pulled the door wide.

The secretary, wearing a pale blond wig that reminded Jo of cotton candy she used to buy at the carnival, smiled prettily. Jo returned the smile, then she remembered and turned back to the attorney.

"Mr. Pierce," she said, "can you think of any reason why I should be in terrible danger?"

The secretary's smile collapsed into the round little hole of her mouth, and Mr. Pierce's hound-dog jaws dropped. They stared at her, silent, eyes wide. She had shocked them, and she wondered why she had said it at all. It had come without planning. Another question on impulse. She was angry at herself now. Why had she said it!

There didn't seem to be anything else to say, so she went out as quietly as possible, leaving them still silently staring, wrapped in their own dumb thoughts.

By the time she had reached her car she began to giggle nervously, then to laugh. People who passed by stared at her, smiled, and went on, and still she laughed, seeing those two faces she had left, both so undignified in their surprise. Her laughter dwindled to a smile and she started the car and drove off talking aloud. "I'd better get out of here before someone slips a strait jacket over my head. Ah, dear old Great-grandmother Stark, what a legacy you left me! It's a good thing those townspeople don't know all we know, right?"

She drove the narrow, twisting, tree-crossed road home, but went on by the rock wall and gate. Not far beyond, the road dropped down a long hill, passed a small house that was probably Tom's, and swept on down into a narrow valley and by a wide gravel beach near the river. She wheeled to the right and pulled to a gravel-flinging stop beside the yellow camper.

She got out of the car just as the door at the back of the camper opened. He had to stoop to walk through the door but he didn't seem to mind. He came out smiling. She put her hands on her hips and looked up at him.

"That was a dirty trick, saying something like that and then leaving without explaining yourself."

"You waited rather long to get here."

"You were expecting me sooner?"

"I thought you might get a bit curious."

She couldn't tell now if he were serious or not. The light in his eyes was confusing. Was he amused by her or concerned? Darn! Eyes too direct and too warm now for her to judge objectively. "Oh, I got curious all right," she said hotly. "I got so curious I took that letter to Mr. Pierce and told him to find out for me."

Loren frowned, a quick expression that was there and gone. "You gave him the letter?" His voice was sharper than she had ever heard.

"Yes, why not?"

He didn't answer for a moment. Then thoughtfully, he said, "I suppose it's all right. What reaction did he have?"

"I don't know. His jaws jiggled."

Loren laughed low in his throat and reached for her. His lips were warm, his arms going tighter, his hands moving. Did he think she had really come only for the loving, where they could be alone? When he started edging her toward his camper-bedroom she pulled away, her breath gone, her control nearly gone. If she could mindlessly do what she wanted to do, she wouldn't have pulled away. But instinct said no, wait, you want more than just a passing hour of him, you want all of him, forever, so now you wait, wait, wait....

"Jo," he whispered, "why not?"

"Please don't. I didn't come here for this."

"Don't you like it?"

"I love it," she said honestly, leaning against him and accepting more for a moment. "But if you don't stop I will never come to see you again."

Immediately he pushed her away, and nearly had to balance her like a limp doll so that she could stand alone. Apart from her then, he looked down into her eyes. But his lips were closed, waiting for her to make the next move.

She brushed her hair back from her face. "I guess I'd better go." He didn't try to stop her. Reluctantly she started to get into the car. "I feel like I'm forgetting something," she said vaguely, her brain beginning to work again. "I know I'm forgetting something. I've forgotten what I came for." She got safely into the car before she looked up at him again. "I came down here to find out why you said what you did. Are you trying to scare me?"

"No," he said, with no hint of frivolity, no touch of a smile. "I'd never scare you unnecessarily. But I think you should be on guard."

"Why? Against what?"

"I'm not sure. I don't have it figured out yet. But I do feel strongly that something is wrong with that setup, Jo."

"Tell me what you have in mind."

"I—" He bit his lower lip and looked at her a moment. "I don't know what it is for sure, Jo. When I know, I'll tell you. Meantime, be careful, please? But don't be too scared. I mean—" He looked down and with his hands shoved into his pockets kicked at a rock in a small-boy way that touched her deeply. She thought of being the mother of a boy like that someday. His son. "Oh, nuts," he said. "Maybe I shouldn't have said anything. There's a possibility I could be all wrong, too."

"Wrong about what?"

He looked up. "Wrong about you."

"This conversation is so clear it's choking me. I wish you'd come out with whatever it is you're thinking and let me judge for myself."

He stepped over, leaned in, and kissed her quickly. "Let me check it out a little more, then I will. Now you run on home. I'll be up later and we'll talk. Okay?"

"Well, okay."

With a farewell wave he went back into his camper and she had little choice but to go home. During the long afternoon while she impatiently waited for him to show up she tried to guess what was in his mind. Terrible danger? Who? The ghost of Elizabeth? She might scare the daylight out of her, but she could hardly hurt her. Insanity? She felt a frown deepen between her eyebrows and smoothed it away with her fingers. The insanity thing was confusing. Insanity was innate, something that would come from inside herself, and he had suggested it might come from an outside force. Like—someone wishing to kill her. Murder. She looked around at her bedroom. Autumn colors here, warm yellows, oranges, browns. Murder in this bedroom? Had murder been committed here before?

She had been lying across her bed. She had told Mrs. Alcorn she was going to take a nap, but had really wanted to be alone until Loren came. She got up and went to the dresser and stood looking at her reflection in the mirror. Loren should be here any time. The clock said it was hours past the time he should have come. A bit more lipstick, perhaps, because the earlier application had been bitten and licked away.

She tissued the excess lipstick, then went to the west window and looked out. Murder. She couldn't get it out of her mind. Strangely, it didn't frighten her, it only puzzled her. Who did Loren think would benefit from murdering her—or want otherwise to murder her?

The whisper came from just behind her: *Please don't make him cry.*

She whirled, chill after chill sweeping her body. There was no one there, yet someone had whispered in her ear! Could it have been outside her door instead? Mrs. Alcorn?

She ran to the door and threw it open. The hall was empty. She leaned over the banister and called frantically, "Mrs. Alcorn?"

From downstairs, possibly from her own bedroom or the kitchen, Mrs. Alcorn answered, "Yes, ma'am?"

Then it hadn't been Mrs. Alcorn. And there was no one else in the house. "Never mind," Jo called again, to stop her before she came upstairs. She didn't want Mrs. Alcorn carrying information to Loren or anyone else again about things she had seen or heard when there was nothing to see or hear. She didn't want anyone to know.

Listlessly, she went to the window seat under the double windows at the head of the stairs and sat down. She felt tired now, disappointed. Why hadn't Loren come? The sun was going down. She had never known a place could be so deadly quiet. Whatever had made her think she would like living so far back in the hills away from people? If she had a family with her, if she even had Dunrope, she might like it. Of course there was Mrs. Alcorn. But something had happened to her feelings about Mrs. Alcorn. A kind of undefinable distrust.

A knock on the downstairs door sent her spirits leaping, and she nearly fell down the stairs in her hurry. But the man who stood there was not Loren Richards.

"Hello!" Dan Pierce said. "How lovely you look."

She drew herself tall and tried to hide her disappointment. "It's nice to see you. Won't you come in?"

"If you don't mind," he said, coming in. "I mean the hour is rather in-between. I would have called first if you had a telephone. Actually," he turned worried eyes upon her and lowered his voice to an intimate murmur, "I came as soon as Dad told me about your visit. I saw the letter, Jo, and I can imagine what you're going through.'"

"You can? I mean—well, you can?" She doubted very much if he could have guessed what had been going through her mind all afternoon, mostly just a tall good looking man with deep eyes, a mysterious character who had kissed her, forever, who claimed to be a writer just looking for a story. Anyway, it was good to have someone to talk to. Especially someone who cared and showed it.

His hands touched one of hers and cradled it tenderly. "If you're worried—if you get worried—I know a good doctor, Jo. I'll take you to him. You don't ever have to be afraid or be alone. Not if I will do."

He was so serious he was depressing. But she thought she saw honest affection in his eyes, and felt her own fill with tears. Pity for someone always made her cry, even pity for herself. He said, "Ahhh," and pulled her gently to his chest, patting her cheek.

"Just sympathize with me," she said in disgust, "and I start bawling."

"I like feminine women who aren't afraid to cry. And Jo," he whispered, his lips touching her hair, "I love you."

She needed to hear it. She needed more than anything to hear it, but from other lips, not his.

CHAPTER 7

His fingers under her chin tipped her face up, and his lips came down to brush against hers. It was a kiss intended to comfort, a kiss as soft as a touch of love for a child. Only his arm around her waist pulled her tightly against him. She relaxed, her head against his shoulder, her eyes closed. She thought of Loren. She would always think of Loren. Even his goodbye kiss today had not been tender. It had been quick and hard, and she loved it that way.

She opened her eyes and like an apparition he was there, dressed again in black, standing on the porch watching them. He was no apparition, he was real, and quickly she stepped away from Dan's arms. But she doubted that it mattered to Loren, for he looked distant and self-possessed as always. A writer out for a story.

"Sorry," he said, not sounding sorry at all. "Didn't mean to intrude."

"Hello, Richards," Dan said glumly. "Miss Stark and I were just going in. It's a little chilly with the door open."

"Oh, sure, too bad you didn't close it before," Loren said, smiling, glancing from one to the other. "I'll come back another time. When you don't have company, Miss Stark."

Jo stepped forward, almost too quickly. "You're certainly welcome to stay now if you'd like. Perhaps you'd both like to stay for dinner. I'm sure Mrs. Alcorn has more than enough cooked. She usually does."

Dan was behind her now. She was glad she couldn't see his face. His dislike of Loren was so strong she could feel it, as if he were a steam gauge about to blow its petcock. She saw Loren's eyes linger a moment on Dan, and whatever he saw brought an instant decision.

"Thank you, Miss Stark. I'd like to stay."

Mrs. Alcorn's voice came from the library door. "There'll be three of you for dinner then?"

"Yes, three," Jo answered happily.

She held the door and Loren brushed past her, his arm touching her and sending a thrill exploding through her body. She closed the door then preceded the two men into the library.

Conversation was very strained and spasmodic. The two men faced each other, Loren unreadable but Dan openly irritated. His face remained flushed with displeasure. Was he really jealous, Jo wondered, or was there some other reason for his dislike of Loren? She wished that Loren would be jealous. He seemed only curious, though. He sat at ease and asked a question.

"You say you're in real estate?"

"I'm connected with my father's law firm also," Dan said shortly. "The older members are all retiring, my uncle has already retired. It's a family thing."

"Connected? You have access to the files then."

"Of course. I'll be the senior partner next year."

"Then you must have known all about the Stark will, the search for the heirs."

"That's right. As a matter of fact it fascinated me. I was the one who kept on with it." Dan shifted positions, crossed his legs, as if settling himself, and fired a question back before Loren could ask another one. "You must be a newsman, the questions you ask. What paper did you say you were with?"

"No paper. I freelance."

"That's odd. I happened to ask a librarian friend about you and she'd never heard of you. There's no record of anything being published."

Loren's smiles widened. "Nice of you to be so interested." After a pause he asked softly, "Did you check the crime magazines?"

Dan laughed, so unexpectedly that Jo jumped. She looked quickly to see if anyone had noticed. No one had.

Still laughing, Dan said, "Crime! So that explains your suspicious actions. I had thought you were rather like Sherlock Holmes. All you need is the hat and the doctor. And the magnifying glass. You probably see a crime in anything you look at."

Loren's direct gaze remained fastened on Dan. "Or perhaps I've developed a nose for crime, like Mr. Holmes. Suppose that could be possible?"

Dan's laughter had dwindled away, though he still looked amused. "More probably you just go around digging, trying to build stories out of nothing."

"Not exactly out of nothing. I usually find that when a situation intrigues me, there's a story to be found."

"What kind of story do you think you're going to find here? It's rather late to investigate something that might have happened at the turn of the century."

"Not necessarily. Old crimes can be as fascinating as new. Especially when they have an effect on later generations."

Dan's amusement seemed to have entirely disappeared. "An effect on later generations!" The words were so bluntly spoken they fairly spewed. "Now you are imagining things. What happened in this house seventy-two years ago couldn't possibly affect anything now. And we don't even know for sure what happened."

"You're right, we don't know what happened, but it obviously was a crime, a murder. And you're wrong about the effect."

"How's that?" Dan asked.

Loren inclined his head slightly toward Jo. "If it hadn't been for that crime," he said softly, "she wouldn't be here now, tonight."

Dan was silent, and Jo stared at Loren. While she was turning it over in her mind, Dan answered.

"I'll have to concede", he said. "Partly. She would be here, because she would have been born here. Or at least close enough that coming here would be a natural thing for her."

But Loren evidently wasn't giving up. "She wouldn't have been Jo Anne Dodson, then."

"Jo Anne Stark," Dan corrected.

Mrs. Alcorn ended the conversation by announcing that dinner was ready, and immediately afterward said, "Getting dark early. Looks like another storm coming up. Table's set in the dining room. You'd better not waste any time getting there or the house will be blowed to Kingdom Come and back, and there won't be any dinner left to eat." She went ahead of them like a white-aproned duck leading her ducklings.

The wind shrilled through the pines and shook the westward kitchen windows, visible through the dining-room door, like large formless hands trying to enter. Beyond the dark and trembling panes lightning cut a jagged edge through clouds that hung low over the trees.

"You're right," Loren said, "that is a storm."

"Don't look to me like you're going to make it home without your truck," Mrs. Alcorn eyed him over the light of the lamp. The shadows cast on her cheeks hollowed her eyes. If there was a sign of friendliness, it was hidden in the shadows. The sudden deluge of rain nearly drowned her next words. "It would take something not quite human to get through a storm like this one's going to be."

To Jo's surprise, Loren laughed and it made her shiver. The room too was cold, being so far from the fireplace. She wished the meal were over.

"Right again, Mrs. Alcorn," Loren said.

Jo found herself looking at him, waiting, but he said no more. He and Mrs. Alcorn now, instead of he and Dan, seemed to be in a kind of contest. Jo decided she'd had enough. After all, it was her house and he was her guest.

"No one needs to go out," she said. "If the storm continues, both of you can spend the night. There's plenty of room."

Mrs. Alcorn began to glance over her shoulder nervously. "I'm going to close the blinds," she mumbled. "I can't stand lightning like that."

Dan had been contentedly eating. He emptied his mouth long enough to say, "Storms don't bother me. Just so they stay up in the clouds where they belong." He buttered a bun and put half of it into his mouth. "But I'll gladly accept that invitation because there could be a tree down across the road between here and town and I'd hate to spend the night in my car." He put the other half of the bun into his mouth and shifted his gaze to Loren. "Be glad to drive you down to your camper first, though."

"There are trees in that direction too," Loren said amiably.

"Never mind, both of you," Jo said. "As I told you, there is plenty of room."

Mrs. Alcorn came hurrying back from drawing the kitchen blinds. "The worst trouble with spring is these storms. When I was cooking dinner, there was just a dark cloud in the west. Now look."

"I hope Mr. Willis is safely home," Jo said.

Mrs. Alcorn snorted. "If you ask me, he's been safely home all day. I ain't seen him around since early morning."

Loren's voice entered the pause quietly. "He always was a bit lax, wasn't he?"

"Lax!" Mrs. Alcorn gathered strength with the storm. "He was downright laz—" She stopped abruptly and turned, staring straight and hard at Loren.

Dan covered a strangled cough with his hand, and followed it with a drink of water. "I expect we'll all be a bit lax when we reach his age. Even this good lady and excellent cook here. Personally, I doubt that she's the man-hater she pretends to be. Deep down she loves us all."

Jo expected her to snort again, but instead she took a kerosene lamp off the buffet and went without saying a word into the kitchen. Dan was talking again, something about real estate, his mood entirely changed. Jo decided he must be one of those men whose geniality depends on his being well fed. Anyway, it was an improvement. He even suggested playing three-handed pinochle.

Mrs. Alcorn didn't join them in the library after dinner. When Jo asked her to, she replied she had other things to do. Jo thought she meant dishes, and said, "Let the dishes go. Tomorrow will be soon enough."

"Not the dishes, miss. Personal things."

She went to her room without explaining, and Jo, feeling oddly put down and embarrassed, made no further attempt to befriend her.

Jo hadn't realized how she had missed having card-playing companions. They played pinochle until twelve o'clock, and when they went upstairs Loren and Dan, if not actually friendly, were at least civil to each other.

Jo showed them to their rooms. She gave Dan one across the banistered stairwell from her room, and on sudden impulse showed Loren into the room of the blue shag rug. She would have liked to kiss him good night, but Dan was standing in his doorway. He obviously was going to stand there until she was safely in her own room. Though he grinned good night his distrust of Loren showed in his eyes.

She said good night to both of them, then closed her door firmly.

Mrs. Alcorn had lighted the lamp, pulled the blinds and turned down the bed. Jo changed quickly to her robe, took her pajamas and ran down to the bathroom to bathe and brush her teeth. The house was shadowed with turned-down lamps. The rain still fell against the windows, and the thunder rolled faintly, soothing as a lullaby. At least she and Dan had one thing in common; she was not afraid of storms either, especially when she was cozy in the house.

She climbed the carpeted stairs slowly and soundlessly. The small dim lights didn't bother her tonight. Tonight she had company. She closed her door, blew out her light, and fell right to sleep.

And when she slept she dreamed. In the dream a baby was crying. It was a very young, very helpless baby, and in the dark of her waking dream she couldn't find the baby. But the cry was closer, closer, closer. And like a dream ending, opening to light, it stopped. That was when she woke.

She found herself staring wide-eyed into the dark, her body tense and aching, her senses strained, searching for the cry. Terror was all around her. The dark of her room moved with the terror like fog over water.

But she remembered she was not alone on the floor. Dan was across the hall, and Loren was in the room just down the hall. The very room where the baby cried. She had nothing to be afraid of. She could get up and go to his room and see for herself, prove to herself that it was only a dream and she had nothing to fear. It was only a nightmare. Without a sound she felt her way to the door, found the knob and turned it slowly.

The hallway looked warm and friendly in its subdued light—almost. In her thin pajamas she felt icy cold. Across the stairway, beyond the banister, was the closed door of Dan's room. Loren's room was nearer. She moved slowly as if a footstep might wake the sleeping, and stepped across her threshold and into the hall.

The girl with the long white robe and the silver-blond hair was near the door of Loren's room, moving smoothly and silently down the hall.

Jo's instinct to run quivered indecisively under the remembrance that she was not really alone. And because she was not, she could be rational. She had never believed ghosts existed, so there must be a reasonable explanation. Thinking this did not keep her from trembling in cold fear that nauseated her, but it gave her determination, to take a step forward, the better to see and understand what this so-called ghost really was. Her legs and feet tingled as if stuck with a million pins, but slowly she followed the girl in the long robe.

When the girl turned toward the attic door, Jo had become convinced she was real. Someone brought in to deliberately scare her? The girl was carrying something, a small bundle, about the size of a tiny baby. But the blanket was black. Who would wrap a baby in a black blanket?

Jo stared at it and her body, pressed against the wall, refused to move. She saw, when the light from the lamp at the end of the hall touched the blanket, that it was not black. It was the dark red of blood, and it dripped down the white robe in long streaks.

A baby's blanket soaked in blood.

Jo felt her hands clawing at her face and heard the screams that escaped through her fingers. Unable to get away, she had to watch as the girl in white reached out and opened the attic door, swung it soundlessly back against the wall and disappeared into the dark stairwell.

Doors banged open on both sides of her then. Loren reached her first, dressed only in white shorts, his hands grasping her shoulders, his voice calling through her screams.

Mrs. Alcorn came running up the stairs just as Dan rushed out of his room. Jo saw without actually noticing that Dan was still pulling pants on. His face was nearly as white as the white robe, his hair mussed, his mouth open in astonishment.

Jo clung to Loren, sobbing hysterically. When Dan came up on the other side of her and pulled her away from Loren she clung to him too. But both men together, warm and real as they were, could not change the horror of what she had seen, and the lingering feeling that she was alone in the world and would never be comforted. She did not feel like herself anymore, she wasn't Jo Anne Dodson, she was not even Jo Anne Stark.

Someone kept asking, "What is it? What's wrong?"

Finally she raised a trembling hand and pointed at the attic door. "I saw—oh my God—I saw her go—"

She couldn't talk. Her chin jumped convulsively and she began to feel nauseated.

Mrs. Alcorn had stopped on the stairs, gaping through the banister at them like a body-less prisoner; she now came slowly up, her eyes never leaving Jo. But then she turned and looked at the attic door. And she looked from first one man to the other. "Did either of you unlock that door? I had it locked." Her voice dropped almost to a whisper. "I swear I had it locked!"

'Where's the key?" Loren asked.

"Downstairs in the drawer, like always," Mrs. Alcorn answered.

"Get it," Loren ordered.

Mrs. Alcorn started to go, but Dan said, 'Wait a minute. Jo, exactly what did you see?"

Jo steadied her breath and tried to control the sobs. "I saw—Elizabeth go down the hall, open the d-door, and go up into the attic."

"Who?" Dan sounded puzzled. "Elizabeth?"

No one made an attempt to answer him. Instead, Loren took a lamp from a bracket, explaining as he did, 'We'll see. Come on, Pierce, get a lamp. Mrs. Alcorn, you stay with Miss Stark while we search the attic."

Jo said, "There's no use searching, no one is there." The resignation and hopelessness she felt was in her voice. She gradually became aware that Dan and Mrs. Alcorn were staring at her. She covered her face with her hands to avoid their eyes.

The minutes the men were in the attic seemed hours long. But by the time they came down again and closed the door, Jo had herself under control. Though she still shook nervously at least she was not sobbing.

They all went downstairs together, then the two men went back upstairs to lock the attic door and dress. Jo waited in a chair by the hearth, and Mrs. Alcorn silently rebuilt the fire. When the men came back, Loren pulled chairs up so everyone would be close to the fire and close to Jo.

"Now," he said, his eyes holding hers to give her strength, or to draw from her the truth—she couldn't be sure which it was. "Tell us everything."

She found herself talking only to him. "First it was the dream, the baby crying—"

Dan interrupted with a forced laugh. "Well, that explains the whole thing. It was a nightmare, that's all and you were sleepwalking."

Loren said, "No, let her tell it."

"The baby crying," she repeated. "I was waking up, but I wasn't wide awake until all at once the baby stopped crying. It was the sudden silence that really woke me. I got up and went into the hall, and I saw her, walking down the hall, her back to me. I didn't really think she was a ghost. Nobody believes in ghosts any more. Not really. So I decided to follow her. It was when she turned the corner that I saw the proof." She felt the warmth of color leave her face. She swallowed hard against the knot in her throat. "The proof that she is really a ghost. She's not real at all."

"Proof?" Dan cried, sounding oddly angry. "Proof of a ghost? That's ridiculous."

Quietly, Loren urged, "Yes, Jo? What was it?"

Whispering, Jo said, "She was carrying a small blanket-wrapped bundle and it was soaked in blood."

CHAPTER 8

She stared into their disbelieving faces and cried defensively, "I know it was blood, because I saw it dripping! It had streaked the front of her white robe!"

The fire cracked and the wind moaned through the pines, but they were sounds alone, for even Loren was silent.

"Tell me," she pleaded, looking at Loren, for only he seemed ready to accept her explanation. "What does it mean? What could it mean?"

Yet Loren remained silent, looking at her intently with eyes dark and unexpressive, and after a moment Dan said, "That Elizabeth—if you mean the one I think you do, it's crazy. The whole thing is absolutely crazy. You've only had a dream or a hallucination. Can't you see that, Jo?"

"No!" Loren said sharply. "Don't say that to her."

Dan leaned over and put his hand on Jo's arm. "I'm sorry. I didn't mean it that way. I'm really sorry."

Loren asked in a demanding tone, "Has anything else happened in this house that could be significant?"

Dan directed a glare at Loren and didn't give Jo time to answer.

"Why keep on with it? Leave her alone. The sooner she forgets, the better."

But Loren ignored him, persisting. "Did anything of this kind ever happen to you before you came here, Miss Stark? Could it be possible that you're a sensitive?"

She felt tired, so tired she could have fallen asleep in her chair. "A sensitive?" She couldn't think what it could mean.

"What in the hell is that?" Dan roared. "If you don't leave her alone, I'll take her out of here tonight and get her into a hospital. She needs to be helped, not badgered." Dan's arm at her waist lifted her. "Come on, you're going back to bed. And you don't have to be afraid because I'm going to sit beside your bed while you sleep."

At that moment she was glad Dan was there, that he had a mind that was more logical than imaginative. She remembered now, as she went up the stairs with Dan's arm solidly supporting her, that a sensitive was someone capable of communicating with the spirit world. She didn't want to be a sensitive. She wanted to do as Dan suggested and forget the whole thing.

But she was afraid now. Terribly, illogically afraid, the way she had been that first night. The stairway was shadowed and dim, and the shadows seemed to move, as a fog moves. And the hall above seemed full of the fog. Even with Dan beside her she didn't want to go up. They stopped about halfway up the stairs.

"What is it, Jo?" he asked softly. "Don't be afraid, darling. I'm with you. I'll stay with you. We'll figure something out in the morning, because I won't leave you here alone."

She went on, climbing into the fog. It moved away as she approached it, lingering just ahead.

He tucked her into her bed as tenderly as her mother would have, then pulled the chair close enough so she could reach out and touch him. Immediately she went to sleep.

· · ·

THE FIRST THING she saw when she woke up was the chair. But it was empty now. She sat up and looked around and saw that Dan was not in the room. Songbirds' voices filled the air and mingling with them was the rising and falling voice of the pines.

Then, the sound of other voices, faint and murmuring, rose from somewhere below. Jo got her robe, brushed her hair, and went down the stairs. The voices became distinguishable. Mrs. Alcorn was talking with Dan. The cheering aroma of coffee suggested Dan was drinking a morning cup.

As Jo crossed the library on her way to the kitchen she heard Mrs. Alcorn say, "I never heard of such a thing. That girl is already as crazy as a raving lunatic. Bloody blanket! She'd have to be crazy to make up a story like that. I'm about half afraid to stay here with her. She could be dangerous. Like that crazy Elizabeth."

Jo stopped, her senses sharpened.

"You can't leave her. What the hell do you think would happen then? I need you to take care of her." Dan's voice lowered, almost beyond hearing. "Anyway, I don't think she made that up last night."

"You ain't telling me you think there's really ghosts in this house?" Mrs. Alcorn cried. "I've never seen a ghost in this house!"

"Shh. Be quiet, you'll wake her. No, I don't believe there's a ghost. I simply said she didn't make it up. She's got me puzzled, but I think she thinks she saw it."

There was a moment of silence, then Mrs. Alcorn said, "Then like I said, she's crazy." There was another pause in which Dan didn't answer her. Mrs. Alcorn's voice held an expression of awe. "You surely don't think she really—"

Footsteps, then, and Dan interrupting, "Actually, I don't understand it. This ghost business—well—there might be something in it."

Mrs. Alcorn's voice blazed loudly. "You just got through telling me you didn't believe it."

"I don't." he snapped in return. "Keep your voice down, for Christ's sake. What I said was—oh, hell. Never mind. You just make sure you take good care of her, keep your eye on her, and keep her away from that damned troublemaker if you can. And let me know immediately if you need me."

"Now how in Sam's patch am I going to get a word to you when I don't have a telephone? A carrier pigeon maybe?" Her voice had lowered but it overran with sarcasm.

"I'll be around often enough. If you've got that coffee ready, I'll take it up to her."

Without quite understanding why she did it, Jo turned and ran on tiptoes back to the stairway. Then she turned, putting a smile on her face, as if she were just coming down.

He looked startled to see her there. "Oh. Hello. How are you this morning?"

"Fine, thank you. Coffee for me?"

"Yes. Maybe you'd like to sit by the fire?"

"Yes, that would be nice."

She sat in the chair he gave her and sipped her coffee, but she was afraid to look at him because she wasn't sure if she could hide her feelings. She had trusted him, but now she didn't know how she felt about him. Was that too a sign of insanity? If she were to the point now where she couldn't tell reality from non-reality, then she couldn't even trust herself.

"Is the coffee all right?" he asked, sounding concerned and eager to please.

"Yes. Has Loren Richards gone?"

"I believe he left about daylight. I think he spent the rest of the night up in the attic. Jo, I hope you don't think I'm trying to run your life or anything, but I think you'd be better off not even talking to that guy."

She looked into her coffee. The kisses of yesterday seemed so far, far away. She had been in love, but he hadn't. "Maybe you're right."

Her words encouraged him so much he put aside his coffee and reached for her hands, setting her cup too on the table beside his.

"Jo, darling, I know this is a little soon, but I want to take care of you. When I was with you last night, you were all right. I mean, you weren't scared any more, were you?"

Wondering what he had in mind, she searched his eyes. "No, I wasn't so afraid anymore." That wasn't quite true, but it was what he wanted to hear.

"Well, I could stay with you every night, if you'd marry me."

"*Marry* you." She had not even imagined being married to Dan Pierce. They had met so recently that she hardly felt comfortable with him.

He looked pinker suddenly. Embarrassed. "I know it's soon. I wouldn't have hit you with it so soon if it hadn't been for this thing last night. But I am in love with you, and I don't want to leave you in this house alone."

"Perhaps I should do as you suggested and sell it. Move out of here."

"Jo, do you really think that is the answer? Remember you said you didn't want to sell because it is your great-grandfather's house. He lived here most of his life without being afraid. I think we could face it together and whip it."

"Dan, what if this thing that's happening to me really is the—the inevitable? The thing that happened to Elizabeth?"

"We'll fight it. We'll marry and go on a long honeymoon wherever you want. Hawaii, maybe? Then when we come back if you feel uncomfortable here, well simply close the place and build a new house in town. Come on, what do you say?"

His eagerness smothered her. She turned in her chair to get away so she could breathe.

"I—I'll think about it."

He started to say one thing, changed his mind and said, "All right. I have to get back to the office. I'm supposed to meet a client at ten o'clock, so I'll give you the day to think. You never have trouble in the daytime anyway, do you?"

She remembered the whisper of yesterday, but she said, "No."

"Then I'll be back tonight."

He kissed her cheek and was gone, calling goodbye to Mrs. Alcorn, who, Jo suspected, had been in the dining room, listening. But it didn't matter if she had.

The morning was gone when Jo dressed and went out for a walk. When Mrs. Alcorn asked where she was going, Jo remembered the instructions Dan had given the housekeeper, and answered shortly, "To find a bit of sunshine, that's all." She hated being spied upon, like someone incapable and mindless.

Subdued, Mrs. Alcorn said, "Be careful of the cliff."

"Yes, I will."

When she walked toward the sunny cliff, whose moss was still spongy and damp from last night's rain, she glimpsed a movement beyond the trees, near Marian's grave. At first it seemed another hallucination, then the figure took solid form and she saw it was Loren Richards. As she watched he straightened and threw a large clump of weeds over the spiked fence. He was cleaning the grave, and she felt oddly grateful. She went over to speak to him.

The small plot was nearly all cleaned out except for one corner. She leaned her elbows between the spikes.

"It's lovely. You must have been working here all morning."

"Yes." He came to the fence and leaned one elbow beside hers, stooping a little. "It does look better, doesn't it? The grass is too thin and pale though. Needs sunshine, I think."

"Probably." There was moss on the stone, she saw, making of it an ancient creature with a life of its own.

"How are you this morning?" he asked.

"Fine. How are you?" She smiled up at him.

"Now that's a bit forced, isn't it? After that awful night we just came through."

"I don't want to think about it."

A moment of silence passed between them, and then he asked, "Why don't you get out of here and go home?"

"Home! I don't have a home anywhere but here. We lived in rented rooms or flats all my life. We were extremely poor because my father wasn't strong. Now I have a home. I have a background. People. Not too desirable, maybe, but people anyway. Real folks. I mean—well, you know what I mean. So why should I give it all up?"

"You have to ask that after just telling me you didn't want to think about last night? What about tonight and tomorrow night? You must know by now you can't live here. There's something in that house that has some kind of effect on you. If you've got the strength of mind to face it, you'll do okay, but otherwise you'd better not try. You'd be better off without people in your background."

His voice was in such angry contrast to Dan's solicitous tones that Jo felt like crying. "You think I'm going c-crazy too," she said, thinking how childish she sounded, and not caring. She felt childish.

"No, I don't. I think you're seeing the reenactment of a scene that was played seventy-two years ago. I think you're a sensitive and never had occasion to know it before." He sighed, and the anger left his voice. "Jo, most people won't accept what they can't see. When death occurs, everything concerning that person is supposed to end. Maybe it does. I wouldn't know. But there's something I do know but can't prove. Thoughts, mind products of the living, are a distinct part of our universe. The thought remains, where it was created, in the air, the room, where it happened. Did you ever think of something, get up to act on it, and then forget what it was? Everyone has. All you have to do to get the thought again is go back to the spot where it was created, and you can usually pick it up again, remember it. You've done that, haven't you. Have you ever gone to bed and suddenly had the dream you were dreaming that morning come to mind again?"

She nodded.

"Then thoughts are there, perhaps for years, depending on the strength or emotion behind them. Well, I think that is what is happening to you. If you left here, you probably would never have another experience so strong it would frighten you. Most sensitive people have only a few experiences that seem beyond explanation."

She waited for more, but he apparently had finished, and was waiting for her to agree or disagree.

"You think someone's thoughts are entering my mind. The thoughts of whoever lived in my bedroom."

"Right. I do."

"Then what about the visual part?"

"Seeing the girl, Elizabeth, as she was then might have so powerfully acted upon the other girl's mind that the image is still there for you to receive."

"Then I'm looking through her mind." She pointed at the gravestone.

"Yes, you must be, since it's the blond girl you keep seeing."

"Loren, what about the blood-soaked blanket?" They looked into each other's eyes, and it was as if Loren's mind was seeking an answer from her mind. Softly, he asked, "What was it, Jo? You were the one who saw it."

She began to shake again, chilling, her teeth chattering. His hand gripped her shoulder tightly. "Easy now," he said, then sharply, whispered words hissing through his teeth, "What was it, Marian?"

She heard what he called her and it seemed right, and she heard her voice answer as if it came from someone else, "It was the baby."

'Where was she taking the baby?"

"Into the attic."

"What had she done to him?" He was prodding, his eyes pulling the truth from her. "Had she hurt him?"

"No!" Jo cried. "How could she have? He was all right, wasn't he? He grew up to be all right! She couldn't hurt her own baby." She was weeping, hard and deep as if it had long, long been buried. Buried longer than all her years.

"Hey, stop." His voice had gone natural. He was holding her, and the spiked fence pressed into her breasts.

"Elizabeth's baby," she said. "It was Elizabeth's own baby."

"You feel sure about that."

"Yes, I do. I'm doomed, aren't I, Loren? I really am." She pressed the wet from her eyes. The tears were gone now, back to the depths beyond her life.

"Only if you want to be."

"No. I am. I know. Maybe it's just as you said and I can feel the truth in Marian's mind. The bedroom I have is Marian's. And the bedroom you slept in last night was Elizabeth's. It's in that room that the baby cries. And the sound of it is awful, Loren. It's heartbreaking. It almost doesn't sound human. Didn't you hear it last night?"

"No. The first thing I heard was your scream. I'm an insensitive brute at heart." He smiled, to lighten the statement and make it less true; and came through the gate, closing it carefully, lifting it to keep the squeak low.

"Loren, you said you'd tell me what you meant about the danger. Was this it? How can Marian's mind hurt me?"

"There are different kinds of danger, you know. I thought that the past, Marian's thoughts anyway, couldn't hurt you. But now I'm not so sure about that. It might depend on how much you're willing to be influenced. I think you should get away from them."

"But there was something else, wasn't there?"

"Yes. I shouldn't accuse without being able to prove my accusation but I'll tell you this: I think your housekeeper has been here before."

"Mrs. Alcorn?" As if she had any other. Jo's dumb surprise heightened her voice.

"Haven't you noticed how she avoids Tom Willis? I think she's afraid he'll recognize her."

"When did you decide that?"

"The first time I saw her. Didn't you ever ask old Tom about Mr. Stark's last housekeeper?"

"No. It never even entered my mind to wonder that about her."

"Well, I asked. Before I even met you, I might add. And it seems she came to work for the old gentleman about twenty years before he died. She was a young woman then. Single. She never married. She took care of him until he died. Then she just faded out of sight. That being about twenty years ago would make her about sixty now. Mrs. Alcorn's age."

The kitchen windows drew Jo's attention. Though she viewed them slantwise she could almost feel Mrs. Alcorn's eyes, watching, watching. Did the curtain move? Perhaps Mrs. Alcorn saw they were talking about her. Jo turned her back toward the seeing windows.

"But why? Why would she come back so secretively?" The bewildering thought of it pushed the other away, and it receded into the ghosts of the night where it belonged.

"I don't know yet. It could be there's something here she wants."

"Something in the house? Then why doesn't she take it and leave? No, I don't think she was ever here before." But she was remembering how much at home Mrs. Alcorn had seemed when she first went into the kitchen.

"I haven't figured it out, Jo. And of course I could be wrong. But the truth is I haven't been able to find out anything about either woman. Not Mrs. Alcorn nor Ethyl Bowers."

"Ethyl Bowers was the housekeeper?"

"Yes."

"But Mr. Pierce recommended Mrs. Alcorn to me. He told me she was a widow. Dan says he's known her for years. I'm sure he said that. He said she did housework for his mother sometimes. Oh, you must be mistaken."

"Then why couldn't I find anyone in town who knew her?"

"I don't know!" She pressed both hands to her cheeks, trying to push away the thoughts. "Maybe she came from another town. I can't stand not trusting Mrs. Alcorn. I have to live with her."

"You don't have to. You could go to a hotel in town until we can uncover the truth."

"What truth? Even if she has been here before, even if—well, I just can't believe it."

"Jo, I'm positive she planted that letter in the Bible, because I looked in the back the first time and it wasn't there. The letter was either in her possession or she found it. Uh—oh, we have company."

Mrs. Alcorn was coming through the pines. She was close, and Jo nearly cried out in surprise. She had been watching the kitchen windows while Mrs. Alcorn had come from the other side of the house. So much for her intuition.

"Miss Stark," Mrs. Alcorn said, and she seemed deliberately to avoid looking at Loren, "what do you want for lunch? You haven't eaten yet, and it's nearly two o'clock. Why don't you come in and have some lunch. I've already made you some hot cocoa."

Loren took Jo's arm and started walking with her toward the house. "I think that's just what she does need, Mrs. Alcorn. And rest. Why don't you see that she gets rest?" And in a more intimate tone to Jo, he murmured, "Don't be afraid of your room, Miss Stark. Ghosts can't kill you."

He went striding away, toward the carriage house and the nearly invisible path down to the river.

"What did he mean by that?" Mrs. Alcorn asked, sounding as fierce as Dunrope growling.

"I think he was referring to last night."

"Oh."

Watching him, seeing him as free as an animal can be, feeling Mrs. Alcorn's silent presence behind her, Jo knew how much she wanted to go with him, to be free with him in his adventures around the world. When she had been a working girl in St. Louis, she had thought money was all she needed to be free. But now she was beginning to see how wrong she had been. She needed love.

Feeling a little like an unresisting captive, she turned and went ahead of Mrs. Alcorn into the dim and shadowed house.

CHAPTER 9

Jo sat curled in a big soft chair by the fire and held a book. Her eyes followed words and sometimes she turned a page. Her mind throbbed numbly, following Mrs. Alcorn as she occasionally stoked the fire or walked behind Jo's chair. When it was too dark to see the words, Mrs. Alcorn lighted lamps. Then she brought dinner on a tray.

And every move she made Jo noticed, and wondered about her.

If Loren was right and Mrs. Alcorn was in fact Great-grandfather Stark's last housekeeper, then why was she so secretive about it? Jo watched her and saw the woman's nervousness grow as the darkness deepened. And finally Mrs. Alcorn began going to the window that faced out upon the driveway at the front of the house, pulling the curtain aside and looking out. After the third time she said, "I wonder why Mr. Pierce don't come. He said he'd be here by dark."

Jo remembered he had said that and she remembered too hearing Mrs. Alcorn tell him she was afraid to stay alone with her. The irony made Jo smile. How could she wonder and be afraid of Mrs. Alcorn, when Mrs. Alcorn was afraid of her?

She suddenly saw Mrs. Alcorn in a new light. An overweight and perhaps not too wealthy woman on the brink of passing middle age, living far out in forested country with a young strong woman who might become dangerously insane—as her grandmother had. Jo didn't feel herself to be anything more than mildly depressed, but she knew that really didn't mean anything. And Mrs. Alcorn didn't even know how she felt. "Why don't you go to bed?" Jo asked gently. "He probably is busy and forgot."

Mrs. Alcorn let the curtain fall. When she turned, her face was filled with shadows of worry. "He wouldn't forget. He'll be here after a while." She sounded positive. Did she really know him that well, or were her fear and hope talking? Trying to sound as if she were just making conversation, Jo asked, "Have you known Dan long?"

Mrs. Alcorn's eyes met hers for a brief moment, then she bent to stoke the fire again. "Quite a while."

"I believe he said you used to do housework for his mother."

Mrs. Alcorn paused, the fire poker held still in her hand. She was thinking it over, Jo saw, rather slowly or thoroughly. Had she forgotten? Or had she never worked for Dan's mother?

"Not much," Mrs. Alcorn said, sending sparks flying with her poker as she rolled a log. "I didn't work out much. Mr. Alcorn never did want me to work out."

"Where was your home? I can't remember if you said it was in Fayetteville or somewhere else."

"We moved around a lot."

"Oh. You never had children?"

"No."

Jo waited while Mrs. Alcorn replaced the poker on its hook and swept the hearth. Then she said, "After Mr. Alcorn died you moved to Fayetteville."

"Yes."

What exactly had Dan said? Just that she used to do housework sometimes for his mother. Well, Mrs. Alcorn didn't know what he had said, so a little lie might help straighten things out.

"Mr. Alcorn must have died rather young. Dan said you worked for his mother a lot when he was a small boy. Probably at least twenty years ago."

Mrs. Alcorn's face jerked up and toward her, her mouth loose and hanging open. For a moment she stared, and the look in her shadowed eyes caused Jo to push back into her chair. Alarm rousing alarm. Then Mrs. Alcorn burst out indignantly, "Well, he forgot. I mean, he's got me mixed up with someone else. I never did a lick of work for Mrs. Pierce until last year."

She sounded so sure of herself that Jo was filled with a mixture of feelings. Relief that she must have been wrong about Mrs. Alcorn, that Loren had been wrong; then a puzzled wondering about the impression she had received from Dan. She thought they had known each other a long time. Aside from work. Oh, well.

Mrs. Alcorn said, "I think I'll take your advice and go to bed."

Jo held out her hand. "Wait." She saw Mrs. Alcorn recoil just slightly from her hand, and withdrew it. She thought now she knew how people in biblical times felt when they had leprosy. "Mrs. Alcorn, I overheard you tell Dan this morning that you were afraid to stay here with me. Considering everything I've apparently inherited and the way I've been acting, I can't say I blame you. I want you to know you're free to leave with Dan when he comes. And to help you I'll have Mr. Pierce pay you a month's salary to tide you over until you find another job."

Mrs. Alcorn stood slightly to Jo's left, staring down at her. The clock on the mantel ticked slowly and loudly. And still Mrs. Alcorn didn't answer.

Jo said, "Why don't you think it over?"

"Thank you," she muttered tightly, and went into the dining room and out of sight into the kitchen.

Jo heard her pumping water. The pump had a rhythmic squeak, grind, squeak, grind, and the water poured out rhythmically too in big splashes every time the handle went down.

After the bucket was full Mrs. Alcorn carried it into the bathroom, and Jo heard it being poured into the square box above the toilet. If Mrs. Alcorn left, that was one chore she'd sure have to remember to do. She wondered how she would feel living in this house alone, with Marian's unhappy thoughts coming in upon her. At least, she thought, seeing Elizabeth occasionally might be easier to take with Loren's explanation of it.

Car lights pierced the curtain for a moment, then blacked out. Jo heard a car door slam. She wished it were Loren driving in, but knew it wasn't. She got up to answer the door.

Dan Pierce came in smiling, peeked boyishly around the door of the hall to see if Mrs. Alcorn was watching, then grabbed Jo and kissed her. Despite a total lack of thrill, Jo felt better. Laughing, she pushed him away. At least he could make her feel like a normal attractive girl, and for a moment she could forget.

"Sorry I'm late," he said. "When a client calls, you always have to go." He rubbed the fingers of his right hand together. "Need all the money I can get for that Hawaiian honeymoon."

Jo laughed again, shook her head, and they walked together into the library.

"Hey, you're not turning me down, are you?" All the bright pleasure on his face was gone. "Jo, please don't turn me down."

"That really wasn't what I meant. Does it matter so much to you?"

"Yes." He came closer, put his arms around her again. "Then you're accepting me? The answer is yes?"

"No, not that either. You said you'd give me time to think about it, but I don't think—"

"I gave you all day."

She put her hands flat against his chest and pushed back against the arms that held her. "Oh, Dan, that isn't long enough."

"All right, another day. Has that writer been around today?"

"Not very much. Are you jealous, Dan?"

"Well, naturally, I don't like him hanging around."

Jo looked up to see Mrs. Alcorn in the dining room door. There was even a smile of sorts on her face. Dunrope greeting a friend, Jo thought. His smiles had always been elusive too.

"Beg pardon," Mrs. Alcorn said. "Didn't mean to intrude. Just wanted you to know I was here." She reached behind her and got a big cheap plastic suitcase out of the shadows.

Dan took a couple of steps toward her and stopped. Jo was left facing his back and she was reminded of school and football days and a player she had dated. Loren Richards had height, Dan had width. She hadn't noticed before how strong he looked.

"What's that?" he asked.

Mrs. Alcorn sounded as if she were pleading. "Miss Stark said I could go back to town."

"What for?"

Jo thought she'd better explain and make it easier for Mrs. Alcorn. Dan acted as if she were in his hire, not hers. "It's all right, Dan. I can get someone else to stay with me. Mrs. Alcorn feels she'd be more comfortable in town."

Dan turned half around so that he could see both of them at once. "More comfortable! What's the matter with here? You've got to stay here with her, she can't stay alone!" It was difficult to tell exactly whom he was talking to. He looked oddly dark with anger, but it could have been the light and the way it was situated below and slightly behind him, Jo thought. "Why the sudden decision anyway?" he was asking. "I don't want her out here by herself, and I can't very well stay here with her." He stopped and took a deep breath. "Mrs. Alcorn, you have nothing to fear. Understand?"

Mrs. Alcorn licked her lips nervously and nodded. "It was silly of me. I'm sorry Miss Stark. You don't have to worry about me leaving." She withdrew into the shadows with her plastic suitcase.

Dan had begun to smile again. "There, see? All you need is me to handle things for you."

Jo felt inexplicably dissatisfied with the situation. "I could have gotten someone else. I don't mind getting someone else."

"No need. A live-in housekeeper is very hard to find. Mrs. Alcorn can go where she pleases when we get started on that honeymoon to Hawaii. But until then I'll keep her here with you if I have to—" he dropped his voice to a mock whisper, grinning, "hogtie her."

Jo smiled though she didn't think it was amusing. "That's rather mean, Dan. What if I really did go berserk, the way Elizabeth did? She'd be alone with me."

"You're not going to do that, so don't even let yourself think about it. Look, Jo, I wish I could stay here at night. Every night. Would it help you feel safer if I did?"

"It didn't seem to help last night," Jo answered.

"Not even later? When I sat by your bed?"

"Yes, then it did. But I can't let you do that every night." Good heavens, she thought. How awful to have someone sitting by to hold your hand every night. Elizabeth was to be preferred. Unless, of course, it was Loren. But she hadn't heard him offer to.

"I will if you want me to."

"That's sweet of you, Dan, but no."

"All right, I give up."

Jo was glad of that. She liked his company, it was better than seeing no one. But she knew the more he was there, the less Loren would be. And it was Loren she wanted.

When Mrs. Alcorn came in to say good night, after Dan had gone, she seemed her old unafraid self. She wore a faded red robe and her gray hair hung down her back in a long braid.

"I've heated the water for your bath," she said. "There's a teakettle of it in the bathroom. I brought down your pajamas and robe when I turned down your bed."

"Thank you." Jo didn't mean to be cool, but it was an awkward business knowing how Mrs. Alcorn felt about her.

Mrs. Alcorn didn't leave the room as Jo expected. Instead, after a long hesitation, she said, "I'm sorry about that, Miss Stark. I don't know what got into me. I'd like to keep my job."

Jo answered with sincere warmth, "And I'd like for you to keep it, Mrs. Alcorn." She had missed Dunrope dreadfully, silent and gloomy though he was.

"Another thing. I was wondering if you'd like to take my bedroom. I would make my bed down on the sofa here. Then you wouldn't be up there by yourself."

"Why, that's very sweet of you, Mrs. Alcorn." The thought was tempting. Then a heavy sense of sadness came into her mind as she thought of her room, Marian's room, and leaving it empty again, with no one there. "But no," she said slowly, "I think I'll stay upstairs. Thanks anyway." As Loren had said, Marian's thoughts, so many years gone, could not really hurt her. It was something else that would hurt her—but she didn't know yet what it was.

"Well, if you'd rather," Mrs. Alcorn was obviously relieved. "Good night then, Miss Stark."

Jo delayed as long as she could. She bathed slowly and read by the fire until it grew black and cold. When she finally climbed the stairs she chanted distinctly but softly to herself, "I will not be afraid. I will not be afraid. Great-grandfather Stark slept up here in the northwest bedroom for fifty-two years after Marian died. He was not afraid, and I am not afraid. He left me his home, I will live in it, so help me Hannah, and enjoy it. I will get used to the memories and thoughts lingering in this house and will no longer hear them or be disturbed by them . . ." Then she took a deep breath and ran and jumped into her bed and pulled the covers over her head. If something happened in the hall tonight, she wasn't even going to look.

As if she had influenced that which was beyond her, she slept heavily and peacefully, and when she woke again it was day, and the clock on her dresser said ten-fifteen.

She felt happier than she had in weeks. She felt young, mentally well, on the verge of a great adventure. She remembered feeling that way after she had heard the fantastic news of her inheritance. The world and life had seemed to have been laid before her, brought to her by the money. Her feeling now seemed more to be generated by anticipation of seeing Loren, of being in love. He was probably somewhere near.

A quick glance into the hall showed the attic door was still shut and probably locked. Well, maybe he was finishing the cleaning of Marian's grave. Or looking through the fascinating old junk in the carriage house.

The day's temperature was already fairly high, so she chose shorts that would show her legs and, she hoped, get a glance from him. Almost any kind of attention would do.

Even Mrs. Alcorn seemed more cheerful this morning. She was humming a tune. When she spoke, however, it was plain her attitude had not changed all that much.

"I see that old man finally brought himself up to get some wood. I guess when he saw the sun a shining so bright he figured we didn't need a fire anyhow. Here it is almost eleven o'clock."

Jo went out to speak to Tom. He stacked wood into a rick on the west side of the carriage house, slowly and carefully. On her way Jo looked toward the tiny graveyard and saw Loren was not there. She looked in all directions, but all she saw was Tom Willis.

"Good morning, Miss Stark. Going to be a warm day."

"Yes. How are you this morning?"

"Oh, humpin' along, humpin' along. Sometimes I wake up feeling like I'd already died sometime during the night, and when I try to get up, I wished I had, and then I think about that old gentleman, your great-grandpa, and how he lived to be ninety-six years old and I figure if I do as well—why, blazes, I'm still fairly young. That always gets me to humpin' along."

"You do very well, I think. Have you seen Mr. Richards this morning?"

"No, I ain't. I reckon he'll be around though."

Jo watched the old man, as Mrs. Alcorn called him, a moment. Then she went to look into the carriage house. The daylight was left behind when she stepped over the threshold and the old black buggy took on the evil proportions of a giant spider. She felt its presence so strongly it might have been watching her with eyes burning out from long years of dust and neglect.

Still, it was only a buggy, and a fascination drew her to look into its seat. She was there, her pale hair drawn into rolls at the back of her head, and she was laughing, beautifully, merrily, and beside her sat a shadowy figure, a man. A man Jo was aware of loving. He leaned toward Elizabeth, blotting her out. The ache in Jo's heart was crushing. She stepped back and the figures were gone, leaving the buggy old, dusty, and shrunken.

Jo realized she was standing with her hands pressed to her chest as if to push away the heartache. It was a gesture new to her. She turned quickly and went out to take long deep breaths of the pine-filled air.

"Stuffy in there, ain't it?" Tom said.

"Yes." After a moment she asked, "That old buggy, Tom. Is it the one the girls used?"

"I think it is. Mr. Stark bought a car in twenty-eight or so, and he always kept it parked up by the house. He said don't touch that buggy."

"What happened to the car?"

"Well, he traded it in on a thirty-eight."

"Then what happened to that one?"

Tom pushed his hat back and rubbed his forehead. "Danged if I know. I hadn't even thought of that car all these years. The housekeeper drove it all the time. I mean the old gentleman quit driving, and when she needed groceries, the housekeeper took the car. I reckon when she left she took it. Maybe she figured by that time that it was hers."

That brought to Jo's mind the suspicions Loren had about Mrs.

Alcorn being the original housekeeper. "Where did she go, Tom? What was her name?"

"Bowers. Ethyl Bowers. I don't have no idea where she went. The old gentleman died in his own bed, up there in that northwest bedroom. And Miss Bowers was with him. The only one. She had him buried in a graveyard in town. The day after he was buried she worked all day cleaning out his personal papers and things. Some of them she took upstairs and put in a trunk. I know because I carried the cardboard box up for her. Some she burned. She never told me what it was. She was one of the closest-mouthed women I ever seen."

"How much longer did she stay?"

"Less than a week. One morning I come up to see if anything needed done, and she was gone, the house locked. A few days later Mr. Pierce, the old gentleman's lawyer, the one what brought you, come out and told me I had a permanent job as keertaker if I wanted it. Well, I did."

"Can you remember what Ethyl Bowers looked like?"

"Shore. She was about as ordinary as ordinary can get." He looked down, pushed his hat forward and rubbed the back of his head. "Her hair was brown. Her eyes—I don't know what color, but glary. I never looked at them any longer than I had to. She wasn't the kind of girl who liked being looked at. She was young, but you'd never'a knowed it."

"How tall was she?"

"About your height. Medium. Heavier than you, though."

"Was she fat?"

"No, not fat. Not thin either. Just bigger framed than you."

"Tom, could Mrs. Alcorn be Ethyl Bowers?"

She had wondered if Loren had mentioned his suspicions to Tom and saw he hadn't, for the astonishment on Tom's face showed the idea was entirely new to him. He looked toward the house and frowned.

"By dog!" A long moment passed, and he said, "To tell the truth, I never paid that much attention. I'll take a load of wood in after a while and look'er over." He grinned impishly, showing a mouth empty of bottom teeth. "Reckon she won't bash me with a stick of my own wood?"

Jo grinned back at him. "She might. Be ready to run." She started walking backward down the path toward the river. "I'm going for a walk, Tom. Good luck to you."

About the nicest thing that could happen to her that day, she thought, would be to run into Loren somewhere along the path. Literally run into him. But she walked alone on the narrow path. As she dropped farther down the hill the sound of the river came to her, water murmuring, singing, eating and chewing at the mountainside, rushing over itself in its hurry to get somewhere. Wasn't that the way with everything? Rushing over itself to get somewhere. When she was poor, she had thought money was the answer. Fight, struggle to get money. All around her people rushing for money. Now she had money. Or at least Mr. Pierce said she had money. She didn't really know. She still ate the same small amount of food. The blankets she slept in were softer than before. Still, she didn't feel as if she had money. Or she had discovered that money was not the answer. Now she was rushing over herself to get to Loren Richards.

She slowed down. Would he think she was chasing him? She could offer him all her money and say, Here, love me. But that wouldn't do it.

She went on, losing confidence with every step. How do you buy love when all you have is money? Her pretty legs sticking out bare below her shorts couldn't buy love either. Sex, yes, but not love. She wished she had worn pants.

She heard the typewriter clattering yards before she reached his door. It stood open and she saw a bunkbed at the far end, built-ins along the right wall with cooktop and tiny kitchen sink, and bench and table on the left. He was there at the table, his back toward the door. If she were his wife, what would she do while he worked?

Wander the river bank, look for arrowheads, the nests of small birds and animals? Sit on a rock and listen to the singing, whispering water?

He must have sensed her presence. He turned before she knocked.

"Well, hello there." His smile seemed genuine, and his eyes followed the curve of her legs down and up again appreciatively.

Embarrassed, she said, "You're working." She didn't mean it to sound petulant, but it did.

He came out, stooping to get through the door. "Sure. I have to work sometimes. I don't expect ever to inherit a pile of money."

"I was just thinking of that on the way down."

"Thinking of your money?"

"Yes. And that I don't feel any different. Just lazy, because I don't go to work anymore. Deep down I'm still poor, you know?"

"You'll get used to it," he said. "When you really begin to use it—for traveling and so on. I expect you'll get used to it very quickly, as much as you seem to want it, and then you wouldn't be able to survive without it."

"Would you like to have a lot of money?" she asked, thinking, it's yours—it could be. All I have is yours.

His smile then was almost contemptuous, she thought. "Of course. Money is power, and there are a few things in this world I would like to see changed. But when I do get money it will be because I have earned it—*working*."

If he had slapped her, it would have been easier. She felt her face change color, and her pride swelled forth to shield her. "I came down to tell you that Dan Pierce has asked me to marry him. We're going to Hawaii on our honeymoon."

"So soon?" The smile was gone. She wished she knew what he was thinking, but it was impossible. She might know Marian's thoughts but never his. "Congratulations," he said. "You've caught Fayetteville's most eligible bachelor. I don't suppose it matters to you that he's been married three times before, or that he was engaged to another girl before you showed up, or that he's fifteen years older than you. Have you asked him how many kids he has from former marriages? And whether he has any love left over for them?"

She swallowed her dismay. Pride spoke up again and said, 'Don't let him know how little Dan really told you about himself.'

"Why should it matter?" she said coldly, hotly, her heart pounding. "That was all before we met. Before he knew about me."

"Are you sure about that?"

"Of course I'm sure!" She turned, tears coming, hot unwelcome tears. She didn't want him to see them. "I only came to tell you," she called over her shoulder as she ran toward the path.

His voice came after her, taunting, "When is the great day?"

She didn't answer. She ran on, nearly slipped into the river where the water had eaten in near the path, caught herself by a bush on the bank above and went on up the hill slipping, falling, running again.

She went into the woods to cry. Into the woods where no one but the red fox squirrel in the tree could see her. After a moment he stopped fluttering his tail and scolding and crept down the tree to watch her weep softly into her hands.

CHAPTER 10

When Jo reached the house she managed to get into the bathroom without being seen by Mrs. Alcorn. She washed her face, dried it hard, then went quietly upstairs to brush her hair and fix her face. Then she changed her clothes.

She'd go to town, she mumbled under her breath. She'd go shopping. Stay gone for several days. She'd spend some of that cursed money.

She went so far as to change purses. Then she sat down on the vanity seat, slumping in dejection. She wouldn't be going to town or anywhere else. She'd wait right here for Loren. She had a feeling that he was the kind of man who'd slip easily and permanently away if he decided that was what he should do. She wondered if she'd be a fool to go back down there and tell him she wasn't going to marry Dan Pierce. Would he care at all? Probably not. At least they were friends before. Dear God, what had she done?

Maybe he would come back to finish cleaning Marian's grave.

She changed again, to blue jeans and shirt, and went down the stairs and out the front door and around the living-room side of the house to Marian's grave. He wasn't there. The tall pines stood darkly close around the rusted fence, and a soft wind sang faintly somewhere above in harmonious disharmony. She stood a moment with her eyes closed, listening. She was beginning to like the sounds of the wind in the pines.

The gate screeched when she opened it. An unpleasant sound grating into the music of the wind. She left it open to avoid another screech. All the weeds had been pulled except in one corner. She found they were large-rooted and difficult to get out, but it was a relief to be at work. With her bare hands she cleaned the ground after the weeds were pulled and brushed away the pine needles that had collected in the corner.

She cleaned the stone too, scraping the dirt out of the carved name. But she left the moss alone. "A green velvet coat for you," she said aloud, thinking of the girl who lay at rest there. It was the first time she had really thought of Marian today, and she wondered why there seemed to be no feeling of contact with her here at her grave where it would seem to be most likely.

Considering Loren's theory though, she thought, it really would be least likely here. Here she had been dead, there had been no thought, no love, no pain, no emotion left in her. Her last thought would be at the place where she had died.

Where had she died? And how?

Jo turned, looking back at the dark log exterior of the large house, the flat reflection of the windows. Where had Marian died? How? Great-grandfather Stark had known. He had been interrupted in his writing of the letter. At night? By a scream? Yes. She felt sure it had been that way.

Why should it concern or bother me? Jo wondered, leaving the small graveyard, suffering the long nerve-grating squeak of the gate as she closed it. It all happened so long ago and had nothing to do with her.

Wrong. It had everything to do with her.

She pushed the thought aside, it made her feel so helpless. The sun was going down, sending long, slanting, weakened streaks of light over the house and into the darkening pine forest. She had worked all afternoon on the graveyard. She'd forgotten lunch and she hadn't even seen Mrs. Alcorn.

And she hadn't seen Loren again.

Slowly she went to the house, washed the grass and weed stains off her hands, and told Mrs. Alcorn she just wanted a sandwich by the fire.

It had been one hell of a day. She hoped Dan Pierce wouldn't come.

But he did.

She got away from his smothering solicitude early by saying she was tired, and she went upstairs and to bed and lay staring at her ceiling, thinking of Loren, wondering what he was doing now.

Only once did she think of the terror of past nights. She turned to her side, put her hands under her cheek and looked out into the hallway. The attic door was locked. Strangely, she had no feeling about it at all, and she wondered if it was all over, if she somehow had lost touch with Marian's thoughts.

She sighed and closed her eyes, thinking, Please God, let tomorrow be a better day.

Songbirds woke her again and sudden happy anticipation filled her, but it didn't last long. By noon she was watching the path, her pride slipping rapidly. And when the old clock on the mantel struck two, she gave in.

She wasted no time along the path. Now that she had made up her mind to go to him again, all pride gone, she hurried. Stunned, she stood on the gravel bar beside the river and looked at the emptiness. Her mind said he had gone, forever, and her heart said no, he's only gone to town, he'll be back. He's coming back at this moment on the road. He's coming down the hill. Hear the sound of his truck. But it was only the river.

She went to the road and listened and looked. She had to go home, she couldn't wait on the river for him. But this time not the path, the road instead. Where she might meet him. How far had he said it was? Three miles to her house along the road. Well, three miles wasn't so far.

The road was even more narrow here than it was on the hill by her house, and the tree limbs stretching over it were turning out tender young leaves, creating a spotted shade. She walked quietly so that she could hear his truck.

A square unpainted house whose gray board sides blended into the setting huddled at the rear of a small cleared place to her left. A thin trail of white smoke came from the stone chimney, the only sign of life. She stood in the middle of the road, surprised. Who lived here? She didn't know anyone lived within several miles. Oh, of course. Tom Willis. "First house at the foot of the hill," he had said. Or something like that. She had seen it before, when she drove down to see Loren, but she hadn't really looked at it.

The door opened and Tom stepped out onto his porch. "Howdy, Miss Stark. Come in."

She crossed his neat yard and stopped by the porch. "I really don't have time. It'll probably be dark before I get home now."

He glanced up as if something about the shadows could tell him the location of the sun and the time of day. "Taint fur. A mile or so. Did you come down the road? Didn't see you until you was right here."

"No, I came from the river. I was looking for Mr. Richards. Have you seen him?"

"Not since yesterday, and the way it sounded they ain't none of us goin' to be seein' him around here no more. He left yesterday. Come up the road just akitin'. I was out by the road when he went by, so I stopped him. He said he was through here, had all the blankin story he wanted." The old man chuckled. "Only that ain't what he called it."

Jo's voice was soft. "He—left?"

"Yeh." He repeated, solemnly, "Said he had all the story he wanted. I ast him if he'd be comin' back and he said no, he'd not be comin' back. He's on his way to Canada."

Jo looked down at her feet to keep to herself the feeling of the world having ended. Loren Richards gone forever from her life. God, why had she ever met him at all?

"I guess I'd better go," she said, turning toward the road again. She didn't want to talk any more.

Tom Willis came down the steps. "I kinder looked for you yesterday Miss Stark, to tell you about that housekeeper of yours."

Jo stopped and raised her eyes. She saw his face of endless wrinkles like a maze, and his pale-blue eyes, and heard what he said.

"I went in with an armload of wood for that wood-eatin' old cook-stove and then I plain out ast for a cuppa coffee. She give me a glare but she give me the coffee too. I sat myself right there where I could get a good look at her. She finally went off to her bedroom and slammed the door, so I left. But here's what I think. Miss Stark. I think she's Ethyl Bowers all right. But I never would have noticed it if you hadn't mentioned it. She's older, of course. Heavier. And her hair's gone nearly white. But I'd swear to heaven that's the same pair of eyes. Nobody in the world had harder-lookin' eyes than Ethyl Bowers."

"You're quite sure it's the same woman then?" Jo asked dully, not caring.

"I'm sure." He nodded several times.

"Well. Thank you. I guess I'd better get home now."

But when she reached the road she found he was beside her.

"Miss Stark. . ."

She stopped again. "Yes?"

"I was just awonderin'. What do you expect she come back for, pretendin' she'd never been here before?"

"I don't know."

"If I was you, Miss Stark, I'd plain out ast her, because I'd say she's up to no good. Anybody who outright lies like that is up to no good."

"I don't know. Well, good night, Mr. Willis."

She went on alone, slowly. Once out of sight of his house she sat down on a flat rock and leaned against a tree trunk, her eyes closed. Mrs. Alcorn—Ethyl Bowers—whoever she was—meant nothing to her now. Loren Richards had gone, and she felt sicker than she ever had in all her life. Nothing else could affect her now.

Not even the dark worried her as it swept down like a hovering bird. She had already turned in at her drive, and the house was near, its lighted windows showing her the way.

'Where've you been, girl?" Mrs. Alcorn demanded, holding the door open.

"Walking." Jo didn't look at her. "I'm going right to bed, Mrs. Alcorn. I don't want any dinner and I don't want any of your medicine. I'm not sick I just—" She took a deep breath. "I just want to go to bed."

She took a glass of water upstairs with her, and brought from a corner in a drawer a sleeping capsule. Sleep cures all, she thought, and swallowed it. This was the bottle of capsules her doctor had given her last winter when she was so excited about the inheritance that she'd stayed wide awake and nervous as a cat for three days and nights and had begun to wonder if she was ever going to sleep again. She had taken only one then, one a few nights ago, and now another one. They might give her a few hours' rest, but they'd never make her forget her love for Loren Richards.

If Dan Pierce came that night, she didn't know it.

Her fleeting hopes that Loren might come back dwindled as the week passed. She thought about leaving, but always backed out, on the thought that if he did come, she would be gone. To pass her time she worked in the yard, cleaning it as she had the grave. Anything to be busy.

In the evenings Dan came, and she successfully hid her feelings from him. Even when he asked, "Where's the writer these days?"

She smiled. "Didn't you know? He's gone."

Dan's eyes widened. "Really! Forever, I hope."

She shrugged. Pride still talking, even when she had thought her pride was gone. "Probably."

"I'm glad of that." His arms came around her and he nuzzled her neck. "Aren't you? Maybe I can get closer to you now."

She relaxed against him, her eyes closed. Strange, the comfort in the arms and lips of another man, when she kept her eyes closed. Even Dan could at least partly fill the need Loren had created.

Her willingness to be loved encouraged him. "You said give you another day," he whispered. "And that was a couple of weeks ago, or years, it seems. Are you ready to marry me yet?"

Why not? she thought. New faces—new places. That was all she needed. She wanted to get away. Why not a honeymoon in Hawaii? You don't have to love a man to have a good marriage with him. Hadn't lots of people said that? More important is that he loves you. She liked Dan, that was enough to start. But her voice answered, "I don't know."

He sighed. "Then maybe tomorrow."

Relieved, she answered, "Yes, maybe tomorrow."

TOMORROW WAS when the sheriff came to her house. She was in the front yard, unnecessarily raking pine needles into piles when the car moved quietly and slowly into her drive. When it came alongside she saw the sign on the door proclaiming it as that of the Washington County Sheriff.

A tall, very neatly dressed man wearing a holstered handgun got out of the car and looked around. After a moment he approached her and looked at a small pad in his hand on which something was written.

"You're Miss Jo Anne Stark?"

"Yes."

"Tom Willis worked for you, didn't he?"

A warning coldness brought goose pimples to her arms. She started to say yes, and hesitated. *Worked* for her? Past tense? She began remembering back. She hadn't seen Tom since. . .

The sheriff was talking again, asking the question that was in her mind. "When was the last time you saw him, Miss Stark?"

"Why, I haven't seen him for several days." There was the day she had seen him down at his house. And the next day he had built a morning fire, and he had kept looking at her as if he wanted to talk to her. But she hadn't really thought of it then. "It's been—" No. He was there the next day too. She had seen him stacking wood.

The sheriff evidently grew tired of waiting, though he didn't look or sound impatient. "Miss Stark, a body was found in the river downstream and identified as Tom Willis's. We're just checking, though we're sure it was an accident." His wandering gaze found the carriage house and the cliff. "It's quite a drop there, isn't it?"

"Yes." She walked beside him to the edge of the cliff.

"Could he have fallen from here?" he asked.

"I don't know." She stepped back, for the first time wary of the steepness. "It seems incredible that he would have. There was no reason for him to go so close to the edge that he would have fallen."

The sheriff glanced upriver, following the huge curve in the valley below. "Yes, it does seem incredible. I understand from people who knew him that he was quite a fisherman. He might have slipped, struck his head on a rock, and fallen in. No fishing gear was found, but it could be anywhere."

Jo went with him back to his car, and watched him drive away. As soon as he was gone Mrs. Alcorn came out.

"Was that the sheriff?" she asked in a low voice. "What on earth did he want?"

Jo remembered her last conversation with Tom Willis, and his certainty that Mrs. Alcorn was up to no good. Could she have had anything to do with his death? Jo turned and looked straight into Mrs. Alcorn's face. "He said Tom Willis was found in the river, drowned."

Mrs. Alcorn's face changed only slightly. She didn't even answer. She stared at Jo blankly, her mind obviously elsewhere, and then she looked at the woodpile by the carriage house. Jo expected her to say something concerning the wood—probably the lack of it—but she didn't. Instead she said, "Old man like that, probably stumped his toe and fell. I told you to watch out for that cliff. It's a dangerous place." She went back into the house then.

Jo told herself it was only an accident. Of course it was. Why was Mrs. Alcorn's identity so important to her that she'd push an old man off the cliff? It was just a lot of silly imaginings. Furthermore, Tom Willis could have been wrong about her too. He might have seen her as Ethyl Bowers because it had been suggested to him.

When Dan came, he brought the news of the funeral. For once his spirits seemed subdued. He was quiet, staring away. When he spoke, he spoke softly. The funeral was the next day, he said. He'd be there to get her at one o'clock.

To Jo's amazement even Mrs. Alcorn went. She wore an ancient black dress and hat. The hat had a veil that nearly hid her stern face. She sat beside Jo in the little white church, and as Jo listened to the sad music and saw how Mrs. Alcorn bowed her head she was caught with remorse that she had ever thought badly of her.

There were many more people at the funeral than Jo would ever have expected. Feeling as isolated as she did, and seeing his house even more isolated than hers, she had never thought that he met regularly with family and friends in the small valley community of the church and the country store.

Conversation on the way home was brief. Jo said, "He had a lot of friends, didn't he?"

Dan answered, "Yes, apparently."

Mrs. Alcorn didn't say anything. Neither coming nor going had she said a word. What was it Tom had called Ethyl Bowers? "The most closest-mouthed woman I ever seen."

Jo was torn between believing and not believing. Tomorrow, she thought, I'll go see Mr. Pierce, and I'll ask him about her. He was the one who had recommended Mrs. Alcorn.

CHAPTER 11

M r. Pierce met her at his office door, his jaws jiggling, acting as if he hadn't made her wait in his outer office for twenty minutes.

"So glad to see you, Miss Stark," he said so enthusiastically that she immediately doubted it. But she answered "Thank you" politely, just as he started talking again. "I was so sorry to hear of your caretaker's death. He was pretty old. He fell in while he was fishing, they say. An old man like that shouldn't be out on the river alone. Still, since a body has to die sometime, going that way is better than having a stroke and lying helpless for years the way some do."

During that soliloquy he had led her to a chair and practically pushed her into it, and then had gone around to his chair behind the desk. Settled, he placed his elbows on the desk, propped his fingertips together, and looked over them at her. He was ready, his attitude said.

She recalled the last time she had been in his office and decided to start with that. "Have you learned anything about Great-grandfather Stark's wife?"

He shifted position a little, settling deeper into his chair. "Nothing. I hadn't brought any news to you because I am still trying. As soon as we hear we'll let you know. I suspect, though, that it was a small private asylum that simply got lost in the shuffle of later faster times. Like the orphanage where your father was. We'll keep trying, though."

"Well. That really wasn't why I came today. It's about Mrs. Alcorn. I would like to know what you know about her."

"Ummm. Nothing much, I reckon, when you put it that way. She began cleaning for my wife a year or two ago. I knew she was a widow and might take a live-in job."

"You knew her husband."

"No, no. I don't believe they even lived here." His curiosity was getting the best of him. "Uh—is there some problem?"

Jo decided to tell him all she knew. "I'm not sure, Mr. Pierce. I mean—Tom Willis told me he was positive that Mrs. Alcorn is the same woman who kept house twenty years ago for Great-grand-father Stark."

Mr. Pierce's hands fell to the desk, and his lower lip dropped at the same time, showing the tip of his pink tongue. Then he collected himself a bit and licked his lips, closing them.

"Well, I declare. She never mentioned it to me at all. Not once."

"You don't think he might have been mistaken?"

He evidently hadn't thought of that. "Why? Do you?"

"I don't know. I do know one thing—that was the last time we talked together before he fell into the river."

Mr. Pierce blinked. "You think—uh—she—uh—"

"I don't know. Why would she? But why would she not say she had lived there before? Unless, of course, she didn't. And Mr. Willis was mistaken. I thought maybe you might know something about her."

He shook his head, his loose jaws quivering. "I thought I did. But now, when you ask me about her past, I see I don't know her at all."

"Could you find out?"

"Possibly. On the other hand, if a person really wants to drop out of sight, he can, usually. All I know is to try."

Jo stood up. "That's all I came for. Please let me know as soon as you can."

He hurried to lead her to the door. "I should say so! I declare, if you feel uncomfortable with her, you certainly can let her go, and I'll have Margie locate someone else. Surely we can find someone. And we'll investigate her thoroughly before she's hired."

Jo thought of her old dog Dunrope, and how in the beginning Mrs. Alcorn had reminded her of him. Nobody could have loved Dunrope but she, or someone who had raised him from a puppy as she had, because he was nearly impossible to understand. Mrs. Alcorn said she needed the job, and Jo knew how it felt to need a job. She was sorry she had even come to Mr. Pierce. Betray Mrs. Alcorn further, let her go before she knew for sure? Accuse her of something horrible just because the poor soul had a personality like Dunrope's?

"No," Jo said. "I'm not uncomfortable with Mrs. Alcorn. I was just wondering." That wasn't really true, because sometimes she was uncomfortable. But mostly, she remembered, since Mrs. Alcorn had become uncomfortable with *her*.

After leaving Mr. Pierce's office Jo went to a supermarket and gathered into a basket all the foods she thought Mrs. Alcorn would enjoy. It might not really compensate for her ugly suspicions, but at least she felt a little better. Also, she thought as she drove home, she'd try to be more cheerful and if she crossed Marian's thought waves again she'd be sure to keep it to herself. To put herself in Mrs. Alcorn's shoes was rather terrifying. Living alone on a mountaintop with a girl who could go, or might already be, insane, was no joke. It occurred to her suddenly that Mrs. Alcorn might even suspect her of having something to do with Tom's death. After all, it was Jo's grandmother who murdered the girl she'd been reared to believe was her sister.

The thought was so shocking, seen through Mrs. Alcorn's eyes, that Jo almost drove her car into a tree. She straightened it out and went on home.

While Jo cheerfully and loquaciously unloaded groceries, Mrs. Alcorn remained silent. The second time Jo looked up to see Mrs. Alcorn staring at her, she decided to give it up and get out of the kitchen.

The day was lovely and warm, but as she stood on the porch looking toward the carriage house, sight of the wood took all pleasure there might have been. She missed Tom. Just knowing he was around had made her feel more at home than she had realized. There too was the faint path toward the river.

She turned back to the door into the library. She couldn't bear to think of Loren at all. Maybe someday she could remember him without feeling she had lost everything. Now she needed most to forget him.

Maybe, she thought, she should confide in Mrs. Alcorn. It might change things between them, make them at ease with each other again.

Mrs. Alcorn was stacking groceries away when Jo went into the kitchen. "Mrs. Alcorn," Jo said, getting a cup of coffee and sitting at the table. "How do you forget a man?"

Mrs. Alcorn jerked around to give Jo a hard, quick stare, as if she were trying to read the thoughts behind the words. "What do you mean?"

Jo spread her hands in an open, helpless gesture. "I mean that I fell in love with him. I never was in love like that before. I'm afraid it's the forever kind of love, and I don't want it to be because he's gone. He didn't love me. So—how do you forget a man?"

Mrs. Alcorn visibly relaxed. Her eyes moved away. She began to stack cans of vegetables in the cabinet, in neat rows, working slowly. "The writer, you're talking about, I guess. I tell you how to forget him, and you can though you may not think so now, you forget him through another man. You replace him. I don't mean to be telling you how to live, Miss Jo, but I've wondered to myself why on earth you don't marry Dan Pierce. He's crazy about you. Anybody can see that. He comes from a good family, too. A family with money. Like you. It's always better to marry your own kind."

Jo was more than pleased with Mrs. Alcorn's response. She had even called her Miss Jo again, instead of the cold Miss Stark of late. "I've thought maybe I shouldn't marry at all. Because of—"

"I know. But he don't seem to be worried about it, so I wouldn't either. Being with a husband who loves you might be a big help anyway." After a pause she added, "What do you want for dinner, Miss Jo?"

"Anything. Whatever you like."

During the rest of the afternoon and through the evening Jo tried to convince herself that Mrs. Alcorn was right. Dan was the husband for her. The minute he came through the door, she thought, she'd tell him yes, she would marry him, if he wanted to take a chance on her.

But the door didn't open. Jo tried to remember whether he had said he was coming or not, and finally gave up. At ten o'clock she took magazines she had picked up at the store, said good night to Mrs. Alcorn, and went up to read in bed. At least she had accomplished one thing. Mrs. Alcorn's friendship again. Cold and grumpy though it was, it was still friendship.

It was past midnight when Jo lay her magazines on the bedside table, wound her clock, and blew out the lamp. She scooted down into her bed, found the blankets uncomfortably wrinkled, and got up to straighten them. The wind was strong and high tonight and sounded as if it were blowing through a thousand wires. At the bottom of the scale was a deep *oooo* that rose and fell eerily. Music of the spheres, Jo thought. And behind her, just over her shoulder came the whisper: *Please, oh my God, please don't. . .*

Jo whirled as if she'd been pulled, and saw Elizabeth standing in the doorway, the front of her white gown streaked with red, her hand holding a long-bladed knife that dripped red. Jo saw her face, the eyes not beautiful, but wild and protruding, the mouth not sweetly curved but open and thinned in a horrible smile. She came into the room, moving closer, ever closer to Jo.

As in a nightmare Jo tried to scream, and couldn't. She backed away, step after step, until she came against the wall. And as if the touch of something solid gave her voice, the screams came, one upon the other. And Elizabeth was suddenly not Elizabeth, but Mrs. Alcorn, running toward her. The blood was gone, the knife was gone, Elizabeth was gone.

Jo crouched on the floor looking up into Mrs. Alcorn's white face. She felt Mrs. Alcorn's hands slap her cheeks sharply time after time, until the screams stopped and she was reduced to sobbing. Then she could hear Mrs. Alcorn's words.

"My Lord, oh my Lord," muttering, muttering, "what is wrong with you, girl? What in the Lord's name is wrong with you?"

Gasping for breath, Jo answered, "She was coming with a knife. She was going to kill me. No, she had already—killed me. I mean, she was killing me. No, not me, *Marian*."

Mrs. Alcorn had drawn back, was moving backward toward the door. "You've got to get help. You've got to! I'll go after Mr. Pierce. I'll go now—I'll be back—don't be afraid—"

Jo saw her run then, saw the top of her head go out of sight as she bobbed down the stairs. But Jo didn't move. Even after the door slammed downstairs, and then when the car started and roared away.

She drew a trembling breath, pressing tight against the wall as if it had arms that could hold her and protect her. She was all alone now with the singing, moaning wind, and she was so afraid she'd see the ghost again. It would be more than she could stand.

Another thought came to her. Mrs. Alcorn had said she couldn't drive, hadn't she? The thought was fleeting, though. It didn't matter. All that mattered now was that she not see the ghost. She was alone and terrified. Too terrified to rationalize or to think about anything but what she had seen.

She didn't move. All during the long hour that she was alone she didn't move. Only when she heard the car stop in front of the house was she able to lean her head back against the wall and let out a long, grabbing breath.

Dan came up the stairs two at a time and then his arms were around her. She clung to him, hard, never to let him go.

He carried her downstairs and put her on the sofa. In a low voice he commanded, "Get her some whiskey."

Mrs. Alcorn answered frantically, "We don't have whiskey!"

"Then get coffee. Tea. Water! What the hell—anything! Got a nerve pill? Bring her a couple."

He rubbed Jo's forehead with soothing fingers until Mrs. Alcorn came back with two pills and a glass of water.

WHEN JO WOKE she was still on the sofa, a blanket over her. Dan slept across from her, slumped in a chair, his feet on an ottoman. For a moment Jo couldn't remember why she was there, and why Dan was there. When the memory came she almost screamed again. But it was only a soft gasp as she pressed her hand to her mouth.

It woke Dan, though. He blinked, looked at her, and immediately came to sit beside her.

"Jo, when are you going to admit you need me?"

She closed her eyes. "I admit it. But, Dan, how can you want to marry me? The way I am. I must be hallucinating and it's scaring me to death."

"We'll fight it together, Jo, as I've told you before."

"I haven't even met your mother." She dared not ask if his family would approve of her. "I don't want a fussy wedding."

"We'll make it as simple as possible. We'll just go to the court-house if you want to."

"Yes. I think I'd rather."

"Well." He sounded cheerful all at once. "You can meet my

mother afterwards. We'll take her and Dad to dinner and celebrate. This evening, okay?"

"Don't we have to take blood tests and things and wait three days?"

"Not in this state, doll. We can be married this afternoon. Look, I'll go wake Mrs. Alcorn and tell her to make some coffee and help you get ready. Meantime, I have to run in to the office. You'll be all right until I get back."

"When will you be back?"

He looked at the watch on his wrist. "Ten-fifteen now. I promise to be here by two. How's that?"

Four hours, she thought. Four awful hours in this house. "If you have to go, that's all right."

"Honey, I have to go sometime and make plans to be gone for a month or so. I'll tell Mrs. Alcorn to get packed and prepare to stay in town too, and to pack your things. When we get back from Hawaii, we'll get a mover to come up after what you want, and we'll move into a house in town. You'll be better there, I know you will." He kissed her lightly. "Now for the coffee. Be back in a minute."

She heard him knock on Mrs. Alcorn's door and call to her the instructions. Then when she answered his voice lowered, and they talked softly together for a while. Jo supposed he was telling Mrs. Alcorn what he had just told her.

When he came back he said, "She's making coffee now. She says she doesn't want to stay in town. Said if we'd drop her off at the bus station, she'd go visit her sister. Said she hadn't seen her in years."

"I didn't know she had a sister."

"I didn't either." He kissed her again. "Bye darling. Be ready at two."

After he was gone Mrs. Alcorn brought coffee and asked if she wanted anything else.

"No, thank you."

"Then I guess I'll go pack. If you want me to, I'll go upstairs and pack your clothes first."

Jo heard the reluctance in her voice. "I can do it, you don't have to."

Mrs. Alcorn didn't pause to insist. "Then I'll be doing my own packing."

An hour later, while she was still sitting with her coffee and trying to gather nerve to go upstairs for clothes so she could bathe and dress, the senior Mr. Pierce came. He drove a long, blue car in close to the porch so that he hadn't far to walk to the door. Hoping he'd think she was wearing lounging pajamas, Jo got up to open the door for him.

"Little cooler this morning," he announced as he came in. "Almost need a fire."

Jo offered him coffee, but he shook his head. "Can't stay but a minute. I was going to have Dan, that's my son, come out, but I haven't seen him this morning. Is—uh—Mrs. Alcorn here?"

"In her bedroom."

He leaned forward and whispered, "It's about her. She's fine. Fine woman." His head nodded, putting emphasis to his words, and he leaned back, his voice raised to a low drone. "I had Dan check it out himself. He said she definitely did not work for Mr. Stark. I would have been out to see you last night, but he didn't bring me the word until after ten o'clock. Everything's okay though, he said."

"Thank you for the fast work. It doesn't matter now, though. If you haven't seen Dan yet today, you don't know our plans, do you?"

Mr. Pierce couldn't have looked more blank if he had made a special effort. "Plans?"

"We're being married this afternoon."

"You and—uh—Dan?" The blankness remained. To Jo's dismay a frown grew and deepened. "Married," he said. "Why—what about—I mean, how can that be? I mean—I didn't know you knew each other so well. Of course, I knew you had met." He cleared his throat. "Where is Dan now, Miss Stark?"

"I don't know." His oddly cold attitude had her flustered. "He said he had to make arrangements at his office. And I suppose he's getting airline tickets. You see, we're going to Hawaii for a few weeks."

Mr. Pierce was up, ready to leave. "Perhaps I can find him there. At the office." He was so eager to go he almost didn't say goodbye. Halfway across the porch he paused long enough to call back, "I'll probably see you before long, Miss Stark."

Mrs. Alcorn peeked out from the dining room. "I didn't know anyone had come."

"He's gone now," Jo answered, closing the door. "It was Mr. Pierce."

"What did he want?"

"He was looking for Dan," Jo lied smoothly, surprising herself.

She walked by Mrs. Alcorn and went upstairs to take her prettiest spring suit from her closet, and came down again to bathe and dress.

When she went back up to her room to pack, she hurried, feeling as if eyes were all about her in the room, as if invisible, icy fingers were reaching to touch her. She packed one small bag, carelessly and quickly, with just enough to take her into the next day. She'd buy all new things, she thought. With no pleasure at all in the thought.

She ran down the stairs so fast she nearly fell, and she didn't draw a deep breath until she was back in the library. She set the bag down and faced the door through which she had just come, and her thoughts went to Tom Willis and the first time she had seen him. "And I shut that door," he'd said to her, "and I never opened it again."

Slowly Jo went to the door and closed it. She stood for a moment looking at the dull glow of the old mahogany wood. Another phase of her life had been lived and was being left behind. She'd never open the door again either.

Dan returned at two o'clock and five minutes later they were driving away. Mrs. Alcorn sat in the back seat beside her old suitcase, and all three were silent. Jo glanced back once at the house, and at that moment she felt she would never return. She had locked it, and the keys were in her purse. She looked out the window at the passing forest.

At the bus depot, when Dan helped Mrs. Alcorn out with her suitcase, Jo said, "Goodbye and good luck, Mrs. Alcorn."

"Goodbye to you too," Mrs. Alcorn answered, as shortly as ever.

Jo forgave her, watching her go. In the beginning, when they had gone together to the house at River's Bend she had not once thought they would be leaving it so soon. She closed her eyes, feeling a disturbing urgency to hurry and get as far away as she could. Maybe they would even live in Hawaii, if they liked it well enough, and she'd never have to come back to the old house.

The marriage took fifteen minutes. She thought as they went back down the courthouse steps that it had had all the fuss and ceremony and emotional quality of buying a dog license for Dunrope. But she had wanted it to be simple, and this was no time for regrets. Dan was holding tightly to her hand, as if it might have meant more to him than it had to her.

So he really had been married three times before, just as Loren had said. The man who issued the license had asked about former marriages and Dan answered him as casually as if he'd forgotten he hadn't mentioned them to his new bride. Oh, well. It really had nothing to do with this new marriage anyway.

Loren had been right about the difference in their ages too. But that didn't matter either.

"We're meeting my folks at five," he said. "At Mountain Inn. Is that all right with you?"

"Yes. You saw your father, then?"

"I saw him."

"He doesn't approve of you marrying me, does he?"

His hand clasped hers tightly a moment. "He's an old-fashioned old goat, but he's got a big heart. It's not you he disapproves of, it's me. He thinks one marriage is enough. Like I said, he's old-fashioned. He can't believe a guy can make so many bad marriages and then make a good one for a change. We'll show him, huh?"

Jo nodded, but then she looked out the window at the passing scene.

Mountain Inn was a hotel outside of town at the base of a mountain. The bar and lounge were rustic, with knotty pine everywhere, as was the dining room. Jo, unaccustomed to alcohol, sipped a drink slowly for fear she'd do the way girls on TV did and stand up to find herself unable to stand or do something even worse like falling out of her chair. She wanted to be able to speak coherently to her new mother-in-law.

It was five-thirty before they arrived, and Dan's mother looked very much the way Jo had pictured her. Neat, soft-voiced, and trim. And distantly friendly. Not until they were leaving, at eight-thirty, did either Mr. or Mrs. Pierce mention the marriage.

"We hope you'll be very happy," Mrs. Pierce said, touching Jo's hand briefly.

"Yes—uh—yes," Mr. Pierce added, standing safely behind his wife with his hand on her shoulder. To his son he said, "Of course you'll let me know as soon as you get back."

"Of course."

Dan sat down again and looked at Jo. "One more drink, okay?"

"Okay. But a Coke for me, thanks."

He smiled, amused. "It won't bite you, you know."

Before Jo could answer a waitress stepped up and spoke to Dan. "A phone call for you, Mr. Pierce."

"Thank you." He pushed his chair back and leaned over to kiss Jo's cheek. "It must be my real estate office. I should have known better than to come here where I'd be so easy to find."

Alone, Jo thought of the evening just spent with Dan's parents.

They had feverishly monopolized the conversation as if they had been entertaining her, they had been that impersonal. It must be the letter she had taken to Mr. Pierce, about the insanity in the Stark family. What other reason could they have?

Dan returned, but instead of sitting down he immediately reached to pull out her chair. "I'm sorry, honey, but something has come up. One of the biggest deals I've ever had is back again. I thought I'd lost it." He was leading her out, his hand under her arm in a way that reminded her of his dad. "I may have to postpone our trip for a few days. You don't mind, do you, honey?"

What could she say? "No, of course not." But the disappointment was there.

He was in a hurry, she could tell by the way he drove. And he was quiet now. The headlights showed a blacktopped road with no other traffic, and Jo realized they were heading away from town. They rounded a curve that looked vaguely familiar, and swung onto an unpaved road that turned upward into a pine forest. Suddenly, then, she knew where they were, and she whirled to face him.

"Where are we going?" she demanded, a cry more than a question.

His face turned toward her for a moment, shadowed from the light of the dash. "Why—home," he said, as if unable to understand her attitude. "Where else? You said it would be all right to postpone the trip for a few days."

"Yes, but. . ." She faced the road.

His hand reached for hers, but her fingers were limp and unresponsive. "Besides," he said. "I really think you should fight this out."

"Fight what out?"

"This stuff about seeing things. We all know there's no such thing as a ghost. You'll have to face that, and accept it, and make yourself stop imagining, if you're ever to be well."

She opened her mouth to protest, but saw the stone wall, then, and the gate. The car swung smoothly in and the tires became quiet on the pine needles of the drive.

All at once the house was there, like a dark wall of horizontal pines, its windows reflecting the car lights like the eyes of an animal.

"Keys," he said, trying to sound cheerful as he opened her purse and helped himself.

She followed him to the front door, feeling too stunned and numb even to voice her objection about going in this particular door. Why not the library door, where she was not so terribly afraid?

He had left the car lights on to show the way, but the hall was dark despite the lights. The closed library door was just part of the dark wall. She heard him go ahead of her and open the door. She was left alone. In a moment light eased up in the library as he lighted a lamp and replaced its globe. Wearily, she went through the hall and into the library.

He kissed her cheek hurriedly. "I'll be back as soon as I can."

"Dan!" she called, protesting finally, frantic with it.

But the front door closed on her call, and then as she started to follow him and stopped because she would have to go through the dark hall where the stairway gaped into the upstairs bedrooms, hall, and attic doorway, she heard the car door slam and the engine start. She ran instead to the library window and watched the taillights of his car disappear into the darkness.

Hardly believing that this ridiculous turn of events could have happened to her, she drew back from the window and looked about her—at the door she had said she would never open again, at the two large walls of old, dusty books, at the big, cold, stone fireplace, the sofa where she had slept last night, where she had finally put her trust in Dan.

Hadn't he said he would take her away forever? She couldn't even remember. Then what was she doing here again, alone now? Absolutely and impossibly alone. Jo went to a chair that faced the dark hallway and sat down, her hands lying limp on the chair arms, staring at the door, puzzled, thinking, trying to understand. Her attempt to think was unproductive. What had Dan—her husband now—done to her? Did he have some outrageous idea that he was doing her some good? It was like curing a headache by drilling holes into the skull.

Her confusion gave way to anger, and all at once she was boiling mad. "Be damned," she said aloud to the silent house. "Nobody is going to treat me this way. I'm not helpless. I still have my own car and I can still drive, and if Mr. Dan Pierce thinks he's going to come back and find me waiting like a docile dummy, he's crazier than I am. He's the one who needs holes drilled in his skull."

She grabbed her purse off the table and started out the library door, then she turned back to the door she had said she would never open again and slammed it shut as hard as she could. The whole house echoed with the sound. Again as she started to leave she remembered she didn't have a light, so she took the lamp and went into the kitchen and looked until she found the drawer with the flashlight. Now that she was in the kitchen she decided to leave the lamp on the table and go out the kitchen door. She was through with the library too.

The dark of the night was pierced only by her small light. She turned it toward the driveway and the spot to one side where she had parked the car.

There was no car.

For a moment she tried to remember. Had she parked her car somewhere else? A flash of memory took her back to last night when Mrs. Alcorn had driven her car away. But hadn't she brought it back? She had to!

Jo began to run, turning her light here, there, all along the drive where the car could have been. She followed the driveway to the road, running, and back to the porch again. The threat of tears burned in her throat. She forced herself to slow down, to carefully cover the possible places where Mrs. Alcorn could have parked the car. Slowly, shining the light to both sides, seeing nothing but dark tree trunks, she went all the way to the carriage house before she gave up. She had never felt so whipped. The anger was still there but diluted again with fear and bewilderment.

She had a choice, of course. She could go back into the house and wait for Dan, or she could walk to town. Fourteen miles in the dark. Beaten, she turned toward the kitchen door, and the yellow light of the kerosene lamp.

She couldn't even make a cup of coffee because the stove was cold and she didn't know how to build a fire and make it work. What had ever possessed her to think she'd enjoy living in this old house the way it had always been? She had wanted a family background so badly that she had been willing to do anything for it.

She picked up the lamp and went back into the library to wait. The clock ticked slowly. Mrs. Alcorn had remembered to wind it. Only nine-thirty? It seemed hours since Dan had left.

Deliberately she kept her mind on the clock. Tock, tock, tock, its voice was so deep and low it didn't really have a tick. Thinking of the clock was better than thinking of her bedroom upstairs. Of all the things she had seen. Of Mrs. Alcorn and Dan. Of Dan. And why he had done this to her. Even of Loren. The beat of her heart answered his name, as always.

The marriage had been a mistake.

Car lights again, at eleven o'clock. The car stopped by the porch. Jo sat still, and after a while Dan came through the door, his nose pink from the sharp night air.

"Hi, doll, how'd you get along?"

She turned her face so that his kiss brushed her ear. He was too excited to notice.

"It may come out even better than I thought," he said. "Anyway, I'm sure it will all be over in a week and we—"

Jo interrupted. "Dan, where's my car?"

He drew back and gazed at her. "Hey, are you mad? I don't know where your car—wait a minute. I guess I do. Mrs. Alcorn drove it last night to my place in town. Honey, I guess it's still there. Sorry."

"Take me to it."

"Hey," he said again, "you are mad. Why?"

"I want my car! I refuse to be left here without transportation."

He went down on one knee in front of her and tried to put his arms around her but she pushed them away. He sat back on his heel.

"Won't tomorrow do? This is our wedding night."

"There's not going to be any wedding night, now or ever."

A sullen look settled on his face. "Why the hell not?"

"You ask me that after bringing me here and leaving me when—when you know I'm—I'm s-scared to death of this house—" The tears came, making her want to cringe in humiliation. She didn't want him to watch her cry. "You can't expect me to want to—to sleep with you now."

"Honey, we'll get out of here as fast as we can. I promise you. Now come on, and let's go upstairs to bed."

"No!"

He sighed. "Jo, you don't have to sleep with me if you don't want to. I'll take the room I had the other time. Across the hall. I'll stay there until you want me. Now come on, get some rest."

"Dan, let's go back to town. Let's go to a hotel."

"I thought it would be kind of fun here, just you and me. Living the way your grandmother used to live. In the house where your dad was born, and your great-grandfather died. And Marian. She died in this house too."

Jo wiped the tears from her eyes with the back of her hand and looked at him. The lamp behind him left his face looking dark with deep holes for eyes, like a mask. His voice had been soft, gentle, as if he wheedled a stubborn child, but his words, his lack of expression, his arms on each side of her a prison though they didn't actually touch her, all shouted a warning: *Get away from him.*

Instantly a deeper warning added—*Be careful.* He couldn't read her mind, thank God. He couldn't know how much like a fool she felt to not have realized all along that Dan was not there to protect her.

Her bedroom seemed now to offer sanctuary. She had to be alone, to think, to decide what she could do, because every detail of the past days pointed to this night and this truth. Dan would not let her leave here alive. It was the money he wanted, not her.

"I think I would like to take your advice and rest. I'll go to my room." He moved back as she stood up. "Tomorrow maybe we can talk." Tomorrow she would be gone. If she could get out of the house.

"Sure, honey," he said. "Here, let me get another lamp for you."

She waited while he lit the lamp, and then she went up the stairs and left along the hall to her room, aware of the man who stood at the foot of the stairs, looking up at her.

She closed the door, pulled the window blind, and put the lamp on the dresser. Then she went back to the door to listen. There was no sound at all. No step on the carpeted stairs. Not even music in the pines.

Carefully and slowly she opened the door. The hall was dark. After a moment she could see the faint light from the lamp in the library downstairs. So he was still there. Somewhere. And the only way out was past the open door.

She closed her door and waited. Minutes passed and her body ached from the tension of listening. Her reward finally came. The footsteps were barely audible. He came up the stairs and to her door. She held her breath for fear he would try to come in. After a moment footsteps, again soft, moved away, and she heard his door open.

It didn't close. She waited. The sound of a long yawn then, and the soft rustle of a bed being crawled into. Another distinct yawn was followed by a cough. A long silence followed that, and her heart beat wildly when she heard the first snore. Laughing soundlessly with relief she pressed her hand for an instant to her throat. Then she blew out her lamp, took off her shoes and, carrying them, eased her door open and slipped into the hall.

His snores were awful—but so much better than his silence. At least she knew where he was.

She went down the stairs quietly, opened the big front door, stepped out onto the porch, and took a deep breath of the pine-scented air. The air of freedom. The stone of the porch was cold under her feet, but she didn't put her shoes on until she stepped down to the ground.

His car was there, a huge black bulk in a world of darkness. If only he had left his keys in it! There was only a chance in many that he had, but in order to find out she'd have to open the door, and that would flood her with light. She decided to not take the chance.

It was dungeon-black in the shadows of the trees. She could only hope she didn't walk in circles. Setting in her mind the curve of the driveway toward the road, she began to walk, still slowly and quietly, because he might wake up and come after her. He would be able to use a light. She didn't dare.

The white in the dark woods beyond the end of the house was at first only a flash. She wasn't sure she had seen anything at all. But she stopped, her eyes straining at the sharp edge of black house against the slightly paler black of forest. Then again something moved. Something near the tiny graveyard.

She wanted to run as hard as she could for the fourteen miles of road to the lights and people of the small city, but she stood, staring, as the indefinable nothing she had glimpsed came closer and became a thing of dimmest white. Elizabeth?

Jo felt herself backing away. She told herself the ghost couldn't really hurt her, but still she backed toward the house, while the white one moved swiftly toward the drive, toward the road, going through the trees, sometimes disappearing from sight, then appearing again closer to the road, as if purposely cutting her off.

The terror was growing in her again. There's nothing to be afraid of, she thought in desperation, but the terror kept building. Elizabeth was between her and the road now and seemed to be coming toward her, forcing her back.

Jo turned, searching the other direction for escape. The path to the river, somewhere by the carriage house. If only Loren were still there! She hadn't time for silence now, she began to run toward the carriage house, dodging the rough bark of trees she felt rather than saw. The sky beyond the trees was speckled with stars, and the light of the stars outlined the edge of the cliff in pale near-black. But Jo kept under the trees, running for the path. Suddenly, then, in front of her the white form materialized, so near now that Jo could see the long white hair.

She stopped, panting heavily, but she didn't scream. Once again she began backing, step by slow step, toward the house. Was there no way out? Was the house to claim her forever? She turned, looking back toward the road, and saw that the white she had run from was still there. Two? Yes, two now, seeming to move toward her, backing her, forcing her to keep going backward, closing in on her.

She forgot the cliff. Though she felt the light of the stars, and knew she had left the dark of the forest, she forgot the cliff until her backward step dropped the world out from under her.

The fall was but a gasp as it sucked her breath away, then her body tore through the limbs of the stunted, cliff-grown pine and came to rest there, her hands clawing at the limbs that bent under the weight of her body. Her breath was gone. She struggled for air, soundlessly. She clung to the tree, feeling it weave uncertainly over the long drop to the river and then swing back to rest against the cold stone of the rising cliff.

She would have embraced the stone if she could have. It was there, solid, reassuring. It and the tree had saved her life. For a while. The tree could still go. She dared not move for fear it would yield to her weight and bend away from the strength of the cliff.

Ghosts had driven her here? Her own unreasonable fear! My

God, she thought, what choice now but to call Dan to help her. Would he hear her if she called?

Voices in the night? More imagination. A beacon flashing down, voices coming closer.

Her thoughts jerked from her and she forgot for a moment even where she was because the voices were real and they were somewhere above her on solid ground. She edged her face back from the stone wall and looked up and saw the light flash through the tree above her. It was a flashlight, and she nearly fainted in relief. She called for help, but her voice died in her throat.

A woman was speaking, clearly now.

"She might have got caught in that tree. It ain't but about ten feet down."

Mrs. Alcorn!

"No, there's no chance of that," Dan answered, driving the light down at her, but passing her as she pushed tightly in against the stone. "She's gone. No doubt. She really made it easy, dumb kid." His laughter sounded low and rumbling.

Mrs. Alcorn, still grouchy, said, "If I was you, I'd make sure before I went to the sheriff. If she's down there somewhere still alive, that'll be the end of you."

"You too, I expect, since you're the one gave old Tom the shove."

"You better not sound so cocky, I tell you she's there. I got a feeling she is."

"Don't be so pessimistic. Even if she did survive the fall into the river, what can she say? She saw two ghosts." He laughed again. "I could have her committed then, which is about as good as burying her."

Mrs. Alcorn demanded, "What about my money? Remember whose idea this was? I've got it coming. That old devil owed me something for all them years I waited on him."

"You'll get it, don't worry. Meantime we'd better get back to the house, get this wig burned and then I'll take you home before I go to the sheriff and report the suicide."

But Mrs. Alcorn commanded stubbornly, "Let me have that light. I didn't hear no scream or nothing." The light began feeling through the branches of the tree again. "There's a ledge right there by the top of the tree, not more than six or eight feet down. There might be a cave or something. She might be there."

"Oh, hell."

"I don't care what you say! You didn't live with that girl. I did. There's something funny about her. She saw things that wasn't there. She might have some kind of power."

"She's nutty, that's all. She didn't see anything." Mrs. Alcorn's voice dropped almost out of Jo's strained hearing. "That's another thing. Do you suppose she actually could be that Old Man Stark's great-granddaughter?"

"How the hell do I know?" Dan yelled impatiently. "I looked until I found a girl without living relatives, who had an orphaned father who could have fit the age. There was no record. He could have been the grandson of the Devil for all I know! I'm going back and burn this junk. You can stay here and fall off the damned cliff yourself for all I. . ." His voice moved away, fading.

But the light kept playing in the tree, touching Jo, moving away, coming back. She dared hardly to breathe.

She didn't know when Mrs. Alcorn left. She didn't know but that she was still there, above, silently waiting for a sound.

Then the car started and drove away. The sound of it was soft but distinct, and there came a faint vibration through the stone wall as it went farther away, along the road to town.

They were gone. He wouldn't have left Mrs. Alcorn behind. Jo closed her eyes in silent prayer of thanksgiving. Could she hold on until the sheriff came?

Her body began to sting as if on fire, feeling at last the torture of the scratches and bruises of falling through brittle branches. Pine needles poked into her burning flesh like ten thousand poisoned darts. There was a ledge, Mrs. Alcorn had said. Slowly, Jo released one tight hand and eased its palm up the stone above her. A slight dip inward at the tip of her stretched fingers suggested the possibility of the ledge. How wide was it? Wide enough to hold her, please God. But to reach it she would have to climb upward and risk the chance of bending the top of the tree out over the river, risk the chance of breaking it—and falling. The risk was too great. She brought her hand back and clung to the tree, wondering how long it would be before the sheriff would come.

Below her the tree snapped ominously. She clung tighter, but she felt it give. Any moment might mean the break that would send her falling. She had to try for the ledge. She tried to remember how it had looked from above. She couldn't remember seeing a ledge at all.

Slowly she inched upward, her hand reaching for a hold on the ledge, praying the tree would support her. She moved nearer the top of the tree though it trembled under her weight, and finally found room on the ledge for her elbow. Exhausted, she rested for a moment, most of her weight on her arm. Slowly then, she climbed onto the ledge and stretched full length, her face to the wall. It was barely wide enough for her body if she lay on her side, but it was a solid unyielding bed. A bed that could turn into a grave if the sheriff never came. But at that moment she was so glad to be able to rest that she let the tension-relieving tears come. She sobbed noisily, making no effort to conceal her place of hiding.

She felt the footsteps above, and nearly too late pushed her fist against her mouth. A light played over the edge, sweeping like a beacon again. Had Mrs. Alcorn not left? Had she heard her? It couldn't be the sheriff yet. She had not heard a car, nor a voice. Nothing but the footsteps.

The light was suddenly gone, and the footsteps too. A long tense time later she heard knocks at the house. Then a voice called, "Jo?"

Loren?

Jo closed her eyes tightly, praying in a low whisper, "Please let him be real." Then she opened her eyes and her mouth and screamed, "Loren! Loren! Loren!" And once she had started she couldn't stop. She sat up, got onto her knees, reaching up along the cold wall. Slowly she rose to her feet. Tears ran into her mouth and she kept screaming. The ground thudded with footsteps, and the light touched her face, blinding her entirely.

"Jo! Jo!"

She thought for a moment he was falling toward her, but then he moved the light out of her face and his fingertips touched hers, and she knew he was lying stretched on the ground, trying to reach her.

"Jo, what have they done to you?" His voice was a hoarse, strained cry. "My God, I can't reach you."

"Oh, please, be careful." She collapsed into sobs again because he was real and he was there.

"Easy," he said, nearly choking on the effort to become calm. "I'll have to find a rope. Please stand still, Jo. You've got to be still!" The light touched her again. "Jo? Don't move."

"I won't move."

She heard him run. A long minute passed but she began to relax. A clanking noise indicated he had found the rusted chain she had seen in the carriage house, and a moment later he was just above her, saying, "I've got a stake and a chain—"

He hammered the stake into the ground and dropped the end of the chain over the cliff. Its cold metal touched her arm.

"I've made a loop," he said. "Slip it over your arms—get it around you."

Carefully, she moved her hands and arms into the looped end and pulled it down to her waist. Moving up the stone wall was slowly and painfully accomplished, but he pulled her up to safety and for several quiet moments they lay on the moss, his arms tight around her, pressing the cold links of the chain into her body. She clung to him, her lips touching his as he told her he loved her, over and over.

As she listened to him she wondered if this were some kind of bitter-sweet ending to a bad dream.

He sat up then, and pulled her up from the dew-wet moss. "I'd better get you into the house and build a fire so you can warm up. Can you walk, Jo?"

"Yes. Sure."

He lifted her to her feet and pushed the chain down over her hips to the ground.

They went into the house and she was no longer afraid of it. But she couldn't stop trembling. She sat at the kitchen table while he built a fire in the cookstove and put coffee on to perk. The clock on the mantel in the library struck three.

Loren came to the table to sit beside her, his hand brushing her hair back from her face, touching gently the scratches on her cheek.

"Jo, what happened?"

"I fell." She tried to smile. "I just plain backed right off the cliff, and just happened to fall into that old tree. I thought I was trying to get away from two Elizabeths, but it was Dan and Mrs. Alcorn. I heard Dan say he was going to tell the sheriff I had committed suicide."

Loren closed his eyes for a moment. "My God. I let it happen after all. I think it scared me more than it did you when I saw you there. I nearly fell on top of you. Jo, can you ever forgive me for running off like a jealous kid and leaving you alone with them?"

"But you didn't know. How could you know?"

"I thought from the beginning that something was up. If I had stayed, it wouldn't have happened. I wouldn't have let you marry the bastard. If you'll pardon the expression."

"I rather like the expression," she answered, smiling. Then, "You know about the marriage?"

"Yes. We'll have it annulled. As soon as we get to town."

She leaned against him. "I thought you didn't love me."

"I loved you. But I wasn't sure about you, or anything. I wasn't sure about my suspicions that Dan Pierce meant harm to you. Besides, Jo, you were rich. You'd been poor all your life. I couldn't ask you to give up the inheritance for me."

"But I would have!" she cried softly.

His hands pressed her cheeks. "Would you?"

"Yes. Oh, many times. And I still will. But Loren, even if I give up the money, there's still that other thing."

"You mean the insanity?"

"Yes. Tonight it was Mrs. Alcorn and Dan. He wore a wig. But those other times it was not they. It was me—my own mind—my hallucinations."

"Not your hallucinations, your sensitivity, darling. You've had two forces at work on you. The human force, which is the most destructive, and the force that is called spiritual. I think you came through very well. You see, I have more faith in you than you have in yourself. I never doubted what you saw."

She shivered. "I'm not sure I like that, Loren. It was terribly frightening."

"But beyond you. It happened years ago. It couldn't really harm you now. At least that was what I told myself when I left you here."

"What brought you back, Loren?"

"You, of course. I was going to Canada to do a story and forget you if I could, but the farther away I got, the more I was sure you were being used—by humans, and humans are the dangerous ones— so I had to turn around and come back. I couldn't really leave you. I reached town yesterday and read of Tom's death. It scared the devil out of me. So I came right away and you were gone. I went back to town and asked around and finally found out, from the Pierces' secretary, that you had married Dan Pierce and were leaving for Hawaii. But I came back out to the river. I camped where I was, maybe hoping you'd change your mind and come back. I couldn't sleep at all. I was looking up this way and saw the light up here on the cliff. So I came up."

They sat together, reliving the awful hour at the cliff, until the smell of the perking coffee drew them into the warmth of the moment.

Jo sipped her coffee, and immediately felt stronger. "Did you know that Mrs. Alcorn—or Ethyl Bowers—killed Tom? She and Dan planned this whole thing years ago. He deliberately went in search of an orphan and found Dad. And, of course, me. The ironic part is, it seems he found the right person. I must be the missing Stark heir. Heiress."

"You're not," Loren said.

"I'm not? But how do you know?"

"I'll show you, if you think you can take it."

She swallowed a rising reluctance to face any more. "I can take it."

He rose, holding her hand in his, using his flashlight to light the way. "We'll have to go upstairs," he said, looking closely at her.

She nodded and smiled a tiny smile.

They went slowly and she was glad. Even with Loren the upstairs froze her, especially when she saw the attic door was hanging open.

"It's all right," he whispered. "Nothing to hurt you here. They probably unlocked it to scare you."

Together they went into the attic and past boxes and trunks to the far wall. The light swept the full length of the wall. His voice was low.

"Notice it's made of narrow grooved boards. Now look here—a hole about the size of a nickel. Just big enough to reach a small finger into. In my case the little one. Now pull. See—a door."

The section of wall, about thirty inches wide, from ceiling to floor, moved out with a whine of old hinges.

"Hidden hinges," he said. "Only the little hole betrayed its existence. Actually, there are four of these doors. Meant for closets and never used. Except once."

His light flooded the floor of the narrow closet, and his arm came tightly and securely around Jo's waist to steady her. In the undisturbed dust on the floor a darkened rotten old blanket still held the tiny skeleton.

Jo turned away and pressed her face against Loren's coat. For a moment he held her, then they went toward the stairs.

They sat at the kitchen table again and drank hot coffee, but she was still so caught up in what she had seen that her thoughts whirled with wonderment back through the messages she had so terrifyingly received from Marian. Messages that now were as clear as if she had been there. Then.

"Elizabeth killed her own baby and took him upstairs," she said. "Then she went into Marian's room and killed her. Great-grand—I mean, Mr. Stark, must have heard her screaming and ran to help. Left his letter and ran. While he was with Marian, Elizabeth changed clothes and left. Disappeared. Mr. Stark thought she had taken the baby. But she had only buried him upstairs in the closet. And Mr. Stark never knew. Isn't it strange that he never knew?"

"Maybe subconsciously he didn't want to know. He wanted to believe the child, David Stark, lived."

"Loren, when did you discover that little skeleton?"

"The last day I was in the attic. Remember? The day after you saw the blood-soaked blanket. I knew the baby had been murdered too. So I went up to search for him. It really didn't take long."

"Why didn't you tell me then?"

"I thought you wanted the money and I thought you might as well have it if you wanted it."

She closed her eyes tightly. "Oh heaven!"

"It doesn't bother you to know you aren't legally entitled to the money?"

"Bother me! I love it. I have never felt so free and unburdened in my life. I think I have learned the most valuable of all lessons. For me it's not money, it's love. I shall make the most of every minute I have from now on. I'll love you so dearly, and so long—"

The sound of cars coming into the drive stopped her. She stood up.

"That will be the sheriff and his deputy, and perhaps some people to search the river below for the suicide victim. And I'm sure Mr. Dan Pierce will be among them. Shall we go out to meet him?"

He stood beside her and gallantly, dramatically, held his arm out to her. "Yes. I think the sight of us will be a fitting climax for his night."

OTHER NOVELS BY RUBY JEAN

1988 *Jump Rope*
1989 *Pendulum*
1989 *Death Stone*
1990 *Vampire Child*
1990 *Lost and Found*
1990 *Victoria*
1991 *Celia*
1991 *Baby Dolly*
1992 *The Reckoning*
1993 *The Living Evil*
1994 *The Haunting*
1995 *Night Thunder*
Pending Bear Hollow Charlie
Pending Cry of the Soul
Pending Pride of Bella Terra

www.ingramcontent.com/pod-product-compliance
Lightning Source LLC
Chambersburg PA
CBHW060545310726
48982CB00009B/1385/J